JAMES CONNOLLY

Historical Association of Ireland
Life and Times Series, No. 11

James Connolly

J. L. HYLAND

Published for the
HISTORICAL ASSOCIATION OF IRELAND
By Dundalgan Press Ltd

First published 1997
ISBN 0-85221-134-1

This book is dedicated to the memory of
Ann O'Byrne Madden
whose untimely death brought such sadness to all who knew her.

Cover design: Jarlath Hayes
Cover illustration: James Connolly in Belfast, 1913,
from Samuel Levenson, *James Connolly: A Biography* (London, 1973)
Historical Association of Ireland, Dublin
Printed by Dundalgan Press, Dundalk

FOREWORD

This series of short biographical studies published by the Historical Association of Ireland is designed to place the lives of leading historical figures against the background of new research on the problems and conditions of their times. These studies should be particularly helpful to students preparing for Leaving Certificate, G.C.E. Advanced Level and undergraduate history examinations, while also appealing to the general public.

CIARAN BRADY
EUGENE J. DOYLE
Historical Association of Ireland

PREFACE

I would like to thank Ciaran Brady for inviting me to write this book and so providing me with the opportunity to engage in the research into Connolly's life and thought that I have so much enjoyed and benefited from. I would also like to express my gratitude for his editorial support and the sympathy and humanity with which he carried out his editorial duties. I would also like to express my appreciation to my family, Bríd, John and James, for the support they provided during the writing of this book, and particularly to Bríd, without whose practical, technical and intellectual assistance the writing of the book would not have been possible. Finally, both myself as author and Ciaran Brady as editor would like to express our sincerest gratitude for the absolutely essential and invaluable secretarial backing provided by Miriam Nestor of the Department of Political Science, Trinity College, Dublin.

J. L. HYLAND
Department of Political Science
Trinity College, Dublin

CONTENTS

CHRONOLOGY OF CONNOLLY'S LIFE AND TIMES

1868 5 June: James Connolly born at Edinburgh to Irish immigrants Mary McGinn and John Connolly.

1878–82 Leaves school at the age of eleven and starts work as printer's *first became* devil, baker's assistant, etc. *accquainted w/unions*

1882–9 Joins British army. Posted to Ireland. While serving in Dublin, meets his future wife, Lillie Reynolds. *First saw poverty of Dub. people.*

1889 Returns with regiment to England and deserts. 13 Apr.: marries Lillie in Scotland. Takes up father's occupation, manure carter and night-soil remover. Introduced to socialist politics by his elder brother John.

1892 Takes over from John as secretary of the Scottish Socialist Federation. Begins writing for socialist journal *Justice*.

1894 Stands unsuccessfully as socialist candidate in Edinburgh municipal elections.

1896 Having lost his job and failed as a cobbler, Connolly finally gets a job as paid organiser for the Dublin Socialist Club. May: moves to Ireland with Lillie and children. Disbands Socialist Club and founds the Irish Socialist Republican Party (I.S.R.P.) in its place. His first writings on Irish question are published.

1897 June: Connolly's first major set of essays, *Erin's Hope*, published. Collaborates with Maud Gonne in demonstrations against Queen Victoria's Diamond Jubilee celebrations. Arrested in street disturbance; released next day when Maud Gonne pays his fine.

1898 Founds the *Workers' Republic*, partly financed by £50 from Keir Hardie, founder of the British Labour Party, a lifelong friend.

1899 Outbreak of Boer War; Connolly takes explicitly anti-imperialist position, siding with the Boers against the British Empire; organises public protest against the war.

1901 Publishes second set of essays, *The New Evangel*, and goes to Britain on first major lecture tour as a socialist propagandist. Elected to Dublin Trades Council, representing the United Labourers' Union.

1902 Stands unsuccessfully in Wood Quay ward in Dublin municipal elections. Aug.: leaves for major U.S. lecture tour, at the invitation of American Socialist Labor Party (S.L.P.).

1903 Returns to Dublin. Again unsuccessful in Wood Quay ward. Internal problems in I.S.R.P. lead to his resignation. On a visit to Scotland Connolly is temporarily appointed as organiser for the newly formed Socialist Labour Party (Edinburgh). 18 Sept.: emigrates to America, where he starts work as insurance salesman and joins Daniel De Leon's Socialist Labor Party.

1

1904   Sends for family to join him in U.S. His daughter Mona dies tragically in a fire during preparations for the journey.

1905   Starts work as machinist in the Singer Sewing Machine Company in Newark. Family moves to New Jersey. Industrial Workers of the World (I.W.W. or 'Wobblies') founded in Chicago.

1906   Becomes increasingly active in the I.W.W.; appointed to its press and literature committee.

1907   Elected to the National Executive of the S.L.P., but growing tension between Connolly and De Leon eventually leads to his leaving the S.L.P. Founds the Irish Socialist Federation—a socialist focus for Irish émigrés.

1908   First issue of *The Harp*, the organ of the Irish Socialist Federation. Publishes *Socialism Made Easy*, arguing for industrial unionism. Joins the moderate Socialist Party of America; its candidate for the presidency, Eugene Debs, polls over a million votes.

1909   Becomes paid national organiser for the Socialist Party of America.

1910   Returns to Ireland, leaving Lillie and the children in America. Publishes two major works, *Labour in Irish History* and *Labour, Nationality and Religion*. Appointed national organiser for the Socialist Party of Ireland (the successor to the I.S.R.P.).

1911   With family (now back from America) Connolly moves to Belfast and becomes full-time organiser for the Irish Transport and General Workers' Union, founded by Jim Larkin at the end of 1908.

1912   As Belfast representative of the I.T.G.W.U., succeeds in getting Trades Union Congress support for the foundation of the Irish Labour Party.

1913   Third Home Rule Bill introduced in House of Commons; Unionist opposition leads to founding of the Ulster Volunteers led by Sir Edward Carson; followed by launching in Dublin of the Irish Volunteers in response. Dublin lock-out; Connolly leaves Belfast to spearhead with Larkin the union response; imprisoned for incitement to violence—released on 11 Sept. after hunger-strike. Plays a major role in fruitless negotiations with Dublin employers and, along with Larkin, tours Scotland, England and Wales seeking labour support for the Dublin workers. Instigates founding of Irish Citizen Army as defence force for the Dublin workers.

1914   I.T.G.W.U. accepts defeat; Dublin workers trickle back to work. Larkin emigrates, temporarily, to America. Connolly becomes acting General Secretary of the I.T.G.W.U. and editor of the *Irish Worker*, official organ of the union. Aug.: outbreak of the First World War; Connolly immediately adopts aggressive anti-

British, anti-imperialist stance; makes contact with the Irish Republican Brotherhood (I.R.B.).

1915 Connolly's anti-war, anti-imperialist policy crystallises into anti-British, pro-insurgency position. Publishes *The Reconquest of Ireland*, a major set of essays on the links between socialism and nationalism.

1916 Jan.: Connolly meets with Military Council of I.R.B. and agrees to collaborate in rising at Easter. 24 Apr.: marches from Liberty Hall to the G.P.O. at the head of the Irish Citizen Army and a contingent of Irish Volunteers, accompanied by Pearse and the other leaders of the rising; takes over the G.P.O.; stands beside Pearse as Irish Republic is declared, with Pearse as President and Connolly as Vice-President and Commandant-General of the army. 29 Apr.: after holding out for nearly a week, leaders surrender. 9 May: Connolly court-martialled and sentenced to death. 12 May: unable to stand owing to ankle wound suffered in the fighting, Connolly is executed seated on a rough deal box.

INTRODUCTION

James Connolly is probably best known as one of the executed leaders of the Easter Rising of 1916. In addition, in what is sometimes thought of as a different capacity, he is acknowledged as one of the founding figures of the labour and trade union movement in Ireland. For Connolly himself, however, his life was an integrated unity passionately dedicated to the liberation of ordinary people through the achievement of the inseparable goals of radical socialism, democratic republicanism, and the empowerment, here and now, of the working masses in a manner that would enable them progressively to take control of their own lives and destinies. The first aim of this book has been to give a clear and simple account of the main events of Connolly's life from his early inauguration into radical politics in the socialist circles of Edinburgh in the 1880s to the militant republicanism of his last years.

For Connolly, as for most socialists drawing their inspiration from Marx, political struggle had to be based on properly understood theory. Consequently, in addition to his lifelong involvement in politics 'on the ground', he devoted his considerable intellectual powers and vast energy to the continued articulation and refinement of those principles that he thought should guide practice. Given the importance to Connolly himself of this dimension of his work, I have attempted in this book to give a, hopefully, lucid but reasonably sophisticated account of the main areas of Connolly's thought.

There have been numerous studies of Connolly's life and thought, many of them written, quite justifiably, from distinct partisan perspectives, and I can say honestly that whether I have agreed or disagreed with them, I have greatly benefited from my study of them. What I have attempted to do in the present work, however, is neither to justify nor criticise Connolly's thinking and commitments, but to make them intelligible. It will be evident, however, from the following pages that not only do I have great admiration for Connolly's political dedication to the welfare of ordinary people, but I am personally convinced that underlying his life there is a powerful and coherent set of ideas which still repays the effort of study and understanding.

1

EARLY YEARS: THE MAKING OF A SOCIALIST

I

Chambers' Dictionary defines 'night-soil' as 'the contents of privies, cesspools, etc., generally carried away at night and sometimes used for fertiliser'; it is almost certain that, as a carter working for the Edinburgh Cleansing and Sanitation Department, it was such 'soil and dung'[1] that James Connolly's father, John, was employed to collect and dump. It was an occupation that James himself was to take up on his return to Edinburgh in his early twenties. In the case of James Connolly, the sometimes ritualistic convention of referring to 'humble origins' is the literal truth. He was born on 5 June 1868 at 107 Cowgate, in the slums of Edinburgh. His parents, Mary McGinn and John Connolly, had emigrated from Ireland, probably County Monaghan, some time before 1856. It was during that year that they were married and settled down in Edinburgh. James's mother was a domestic servant, while his father, as we have seen, worked all his life for the Cleansing and Sanitation Department of Edinburgh. He had two older brothers: John, four years his senior, was to be influential in leading James into socialism; Thomas, born two years before James, trained as a compositor's assistant and seems to have emigrated, little else being known about him.

Connolly received a basic primary education in the Catholic school of St Patrick's in the Cowgate district, but by the age of eleven he had left school to take up a full-time job. He worked first as a 'printer's devil', then as an assistant in a bakery, and later in a tile and mosaic factory. When, at the age of fourteen, he was finding it more difficult to get work, he followed his brother John, falsified his age and joined the army, enlisting in the Royal Scots Regiment. Few details are known about his army career, but it is certain that it was as a member of the army that Connolly first visited Ireland, being posted first in the Cork area and then around Dublin. It was during his stay in Dublin in 1888 that he met his future wife, Lillie Reynolds. They were both waiting for the tram to Kingstown (Dún Laoire) in Merrion Square. When the tram failed to stop, they fell into conversation. They quickly became friends and by the end of 1888 had decided to get married. Lillie was from a County Wicklow Protestant family and was working at the time as a domestic servant in Dublin. She was to remain with James after their marriage for the rest of his life. Some time in 1889 Connolly's regiment returned to England, apparently in preparation for being posted abroad. Though James had only a few months of his seven-year enlistment to serve, he decided, for whatever reasons, to desert and make his way back to Scotland. Lillie travelled over from Ireland and they eventually were married on 20 April in St John's Church in Perth, though they settled in Edinburgh, where James had, along with his brother John, taken up his father's occupation as a carter working for the Cleansing and Sanitation Department.

Whether Connolly's interest in politics predated his return to Edinburgh is not known; what is known is that literally within weeks of his taking up a job of carter in that city his feet were firmly placed on the path of labour struggles and socialist politics that was to define the rest of his life. In April 1889 he described himself and his brother as ringleaders of a planned strike among the carters, his brother already being active in socialist politics.

From the seventeenth century onwards England had led the world in the development of a modern commercial, capitalistic, industrialised economy, and in so doing created the first urban industrial proletariat—the working class. While there had been periods of organised militancy, notably the Chartist campaigns of the 1830s and 1840s, by and large the working class had looked to progressive elements of already established political parties, particularly the Liberal Party, for the representation of its interests. Only towards the end of the century, in the 1880s, was there a serious attempt to create an organisation that would represent the working class directly. James Keir Hardie, with whom Connolly was to form a lifelong friendship, founded what was to become the Independent Labour Party and, in 1892, became the first Labour member of parliament at Westminster, winning the seat for West Ham. While many supporters of the Labour movement were relatively moderate in their political beliefs, some became progressively influenced by the radical socialist theories of, among others, Karl Marx and Friedrich Engels. Though first Engels and then Marx had been permanent residents in England since the middle of the nineteenth century, their influence at first was limited to German émigré groups. Only after Marx's death in 1883 did his influence begin to grow in British socialist organisations such as H. M. Hyndman's Social Democratic Federation (S.D.F.), William Morris's breakaway Socialist League, and the Scottish Socialist Federation (S.S.F.), founded by John Leslie, with which Connolly was to become associated in 1889. From that time on, Connolly's life began to revolve almost entirely around socialist politics. (help workers)

When, in 1892, he took over from his brother John as secretary of the S.S.F., he became the very epitome of the radical committed socialist. He strove to educate himself in the socialist classics, he became a street-corner agitator, he lectured on Marxist economic theory to his less-informed colleagues, he ran the affairs of the S.S.F., stood, unsuccessfully, several times in local elections, wrote notes for *Justice* (the S.D.F. journal) and began publishing a regular column of acerbic political comments under the jocular pseudonym of 'R. Ascal' in the *Edinburgh and Leith Chronicle*. His home became the focal point for administration and educational meetings of Edinburgh socialists. Of course, his ordinary life did go on. His first three children, Mona, Nora and Aideen, were born between 1890 and 1896. He continued working as a carter until he was refused work in 1894, possibly as a result of his growing radical reputation. When his attempt to set himself up as a self-employed cobbler failed, his economic situation became desperate. He even made tentative inquiries about emigrating to Chile. From 1895 he also began to seek paid employment in the socialist movement, and eventually in 1896, after an appeal in *Justice* on his behalf by John Leslie, he was offered the position of organiser by the Dublin Socialist Club at the salary of £1 per week. In the 1890s the socalist movement in Ireland was far from strong, and the Dublin Socialist Club was in effect a small loose organisation with few members, the most prominent being Robert Dorman, Thomas, Daniel and William

O'Brien and J. T. Lyng. It was to work on this fallow ground that
Connolly, in May 1896, left Edinburgh to take the socialist gospel
to Ireland.

II

The question of the nature of Connolly's socialism and the
depth and genuineness of his Marxism have been contentious
issues. Paradoxically, his Marxism has been challenged from both
the left and the right,[2] most famously and extremely by Lambert
McKenna, S.J., in a pamphlet originally published in 1920.
McKenna did not deny Connolly's unswerving commitment to a
socialist society, but set out to argue that Connolly was first and
foremost a Fenian, inspired by a love of Ireland, and that lacking
academic education, theoretical ability and time, he allowed
himself to become befuddled by the esoteric doctrines of a
German philosophy. The result, according to McKenna, was that
Connolly himself did not hold with most of the central tenets of
Marxism.[3] The question of just how much of a Marxist Connolly
was is rendered somewhat complicated because, firstly, there are
many different aspects of Marx's thought and, secondly, it is not
self-evidently true that there is a single unambiguous answer to
the question of what the really essential and fundamental
elements of Marxism are.

To begin with, however, it should be emphasised that, from
Connolly's earliest involvement in the socialist movement, both
he and his closest colleagues considered him a thoroughgoing
Marxist. He unequivocally refers to Marx as 'the greatest of
modern thinkers',[4] and his language is redolent with Marxist
terminology. *Justice* on 30 May 1896 gave the following description
of his economic classes for S.D.F. members: 'The gospel
according to Marx is then and there expounded by Connolly, and
needless to say, his exegesis is the authoritative one . . . free from
dilution or adulteration.'[5] Of course, if none of the parties
involved had a really accurate knowledge of the essentials of
Marxism, we could still, as McKenna suggests, be dealing with a
case of mis-identification.

Fundamentally, socialism is that form of society in which the wealth-producing assets of the community are vested in the community itself and in which the organisation of the production and distribution of goods and services is also under the direct control of the community. There is no doubt that it was to this form of unambiguous democratic socialism that Connolly was committed, whether he called it a workers' republic, the working-class democracy, an industrial commonwealth, or simply socialism. He was implacably opposed to capitalist private property in the means of production and was unswervingly committed to an egalitarian democratic control of economic production and distribution. Connolly himself always insisted on distinguishing between an individual's socialism as, fundamentally, their commitment to this common ownership of the means of production and any other aspects of their values or beliefs. As he put it in *Labour, Nationality and Religion,*

> Socialists are bound as socialists only to the acceptance of one great principle—the ownership and control of wealth-producing power by the state, and that, therefore, totally antagonistic interpretations of the Bible, or of prophecy and revelation, theories of marriage and of history may be held by socialists without in the slightest degree interfering with their activities as such or with their proper classification as supporters of socialist doctrine.[6]

When we move on to the ideology of radical socialism identified with Marx himself, matters become a little more complicated. Logically, there could be many different reasons why different people might be committed to socialism in the first sense of the term. But there is a distinctive analysis of capitalist society that constitutes the radical socialism being referred to here, and it is an analysis that is central to the *Marxist* commitment to socialism. Although dispute is possible concerning the essential elements of this analysis, I would suggest that the following five factors are central. Firstly, there is the unconditional rejection of any possible justification of private property in the means of production. Again, on this matter there is no doubt whatsoever that this was Connolly's position. He quotes with evident glee, in his polemic with Father Kane, S.J., from some of the early Christian patristic writers where they anticipate Proudhon in declaring private

property to be theft.[7] The second element of radical socialism
consists in the claim that capitalist profit derives exclusively from
the exploitation of labour. We might say that this thesis has both a
general and a technical form, both of which Connolly endorses. A
good example of the former, claiming that capitalists simply live
off the labour of the working class, can be found in the short
article 'Let Us Free Ireland' published in the *Workers' Republic* of
1899, in which he says:

> The capitalist, I say, is a parasite on industry; as useless in the
> present stage of our industrial development as any other
> parasite in the animal or vegetable world is to the life of the
> animal or vegetable upon which it feeds. The working class is
> the victim of this parasite—this human leech, and it is the
> duty and interest of the working class to use every means in its
> power to oust this parasite class from the position which
> enables it to thus prey upon the vitals of labour.[8]

The more technical form of the thesis consists in Marx's famous
Labour Theory of Value, on the basis of which classical Marxism
argued that, as a matter of economic law, the profit that is
generated in a capitalist economy derives exclusively from the
technical exploitation of labour. Marx took it as a scientifically
demonstrable fact that capitalist profit arose solely from forcing
workers to engage in surplus labour over and above the labour
required to produce their own consumption needs, this surplus
labour being the basis of what he defined as the 'the rate of
exploitation'[9] Although in his writings Connolly nowhere gives an
extended account of this theory, there is no doubt that it was for
him the basis of what he thought of as 'scientific socialism'. In
Labour, Nationality and Religion we find the following: 'The exposi-
tion of the true nature of capital, viz., that it is stored-up, unpaid
labour, forms the very basis of the Socialist criticism of modern
society, and its method of wealth production; it is the fundamental idea of modern Marxist Socialism.'[10] A little further on he
produces a word-perfect accurate account of the basic labour
theory of value underlying the theory of capitalist exploitation
when he claims that 'the amount of labour necessary to produce
an article under average social conditions governs its exchange
value'.[11] Whatever about Connolly's critical grasp of the more
esoteric aspects of Marx's economic analysis of capitalism, there

can be no uncertainty concerning his acceptance of the basics of that analysis in the labour theory of value and the explanation of profit as arising from exploitation.

It is in this uncompromising analysis of the basis of capitalist wealth that the third, fourth and fifth elements of the ideology of radical socialism are grounded. The third of these consists of the proposition that Marxists do not see social inequality as consisting simply in the fact that some people are better off than others. The wealth of the rich is rooted in their exploitation of the poor; hence, for Marxists, the two groups constitute radically opposed 'antagonistic classes'.[12] Fourthly, the exploited working class is justified, as we saw Connolly saying above, in using 'every means in its power to oust this parasite class'.[13] Connolly was to take up the issue of physical force and revolutionary violence many times in his writings, and his position is absolutely clear: though not committed to revolutionary violence for its own sake, and though convinced that in most circumstances it will be of only secondary importance, revolutionary violence is justified if necessary. For example, in an early article in the *Workers' Republic* on 22 July 1899 Connolly says:

> If the time should arrive when the party of progress finds its way to freedom barred by the stubborn greed of a possessing class entrenched behind the barriers of law and order; if the party of progress has indoctrinated the people at large with the new revolutionary conception of society and is therefore representative of the will of a majority of the nation; if it has exhausted all the peaceful means at its disposal for the purpose of demonstrating to the people and their enemies that the new revolutionary ideas do possess the suffrage of the majority; then, but not till then, the party which represents the revolutionary idea is justified in taking steps to assume the powers of government, and in using the weapons of force to dislodge the usurping class.[14]

Fifthly and finally, essential to the Marxist concept of revolutionary socialism is the thesis that the liberation of the workers must ultimately lie in their own hands. As we shall see when we come to Connolly's conception of industrial unionism in the next chapter, he not only accepted the thesis of self-liberation generally, but developed a particular detailed interpretation of it in which revolutionary power and organisation were to grow out of a

particular form of trade unionism. Connolly was unequivocally a
revolutionary socialist, accepting without reservation the central
tenets of the ideology of radical socialism.

But did he, in more general terms, accept wholesale the
theories of Marx? In particular, did he espouse the Marxist theory
of history known as historical materialism and Marx's more wide-
ranging philosophical views on, in particular, religion and
morality?

In its technical detail, historical materialism or 'the materialist
conception of history', as it is sometimes called, is a complete set
of theories concerning the fundamental factors that determine
the institutional order of a society and its transformation over
time. We can summarise the essential thesis in the words that
Connolly himself approvingly uses:

> That in every historical epoch the prevailing method of
> economic production and exchange, and the social organisa-
> tion necessarily following from it, forms the basis upon which
> alone can be explained the political and intellectual history
> of that epoch.[15]

What is being claimed here is that every historical epoch is
characterised by a dominant economic system such as slavery,
feudalism or capitalism, and that all the significant features of the
other dimensions of the institutional order of society are to be
explained solely by reference to the economic system. Thus the
forms of religion and morality, the institutions of marriage and
the family in some particular period, the structure of the state
and the constitution of political power, among other things, are to
be explained in terms of the form of economic production and
distribution and the consequent type of economic exploitation
that characterise a particular society.

In addition to this static analysis of a society in 'equilibrium',
the theory postulates a specific dynamism to human history, a
tendency for the productive technology to be developed and
hence to render obsolete and unstable previous forms of property
in the forces of production and systems of exploitation. It is this
aspect of the theory that Connolly was alluding to in the passage
from 'Let Us Free Ireland' quoted above, when he describes the
capitalist parasite as 'useless in the present stage of our industrial

development'.[16] It is also this that lies behind his somewhat wry story explaining the demise of slavery in *Labour, Nationality and Religion*, which concludes with the moral: 'Slavery is immoral because slaves cost too much.'[17] Connolly also clearly endorsed what we would call the social-psychological underpinnings of the theory in the simple formulation of the thesis that we also find in *Labour, Nationality and Religion*, where he claims that

> the ideas of men are derived from their material surroundings, and that the forces which made and make for historical changes and human progress had and have their roots in the development of the tools men have used in their struggle for existence, using the word 'tools' in its broadest possible sense to include all the social forces of wealth-production.[18]

It is only when we turn to the more wide-ranging philosophical theories of Marx concerning morality and religion that we find Connolly significantly diverging from Marx in theory and practice. From his earliest involvement with the Young Hegelian movement in the 1830s Marx was committed to the 'critique of religion' and adopted what could only be called an outspoken aggressive atheism and a moral nihilism that explicitly denied any validity to the idea that there were universally valid categorical moral rules according to which human beings should order their lives.[19] A more extended discussion of Connolly's views on religion and morality will be offered in the next chapter in the context of the debate that occurred between him and the American socialist Daniel De Leon in 1904. But we can here make two general observations: firstly, that he continued to use straightforwardly the moral language of duty, obligation and right; and secondly, that although he would often attack particular representatives of religion for their political stances, as in *Labour, Nationality and Religion*,[20] he never attacked religion as such. This was probably motivated in part theoretically and in part pragmatically. Levenson refers to Connolly as having said: 'We cannot undertake to correct all errors because we are not the possessors of all knowledge.'[21] Connolly's pragmatic position is, however, abundantly clear. Pragmatic as it is, it is more than opportunism, having a clear principled basis in Connolly's thought. He clearly believed that a genuine and unswerving commitment to socialism as a form of society was compatible with a wide variety of religious and non-religious beliefs; it was even compatible with the non-acceptance of the Marxist theory of exploitation and historical materialism. As a consequence, if one's central practical goal is the revolutionary overthrow of capitalism and the achievement of a democratic socialist republic, people's religious beliefs, so long as they do not lead to a rejection of socialism, are of no concern to the struggle. And it was precisely a commitment to this political battle for a workers' republic that Connolly brought to Dublin with him in 1896.

2

DUBLIN, 1896–1903: REPUBLICAN SOCIALISM

I

Connolly's first move on arriving in Dublin was to disband the Socialist Club and to establish in its place the Irish Socialist Republican Party. Along with Connolly were seven other founder members, justifying the literal truth of a quip popular in Dublin at the time that it was the only party with more syllables in its name than members. Connolly's manifesto for the party which he published in September 1896 was progressive and radical, demanding the immediate nationalisation of railways, canals and banks, the introduction of a graduated income tax, a minimum wage, a forty-eight-hour week, free child care, free education up to university level, public control of schools, universal suffrage and a socialist commitment to the gradual extension of public ownership.[1] To earn his £1 per week he threw himself with characteristic vigour into the organisational and propaganda work of the party. He initiated a series of public propaganda meetings outside the Custom House and, a short time later, in the Phoenix Park on Sundays.

In the offices that the party had secured at 67 Middle Abbey Street he held educational meetings for the party members. He himself began serious research into Irish social history and the writings of earlier radicals. In particular, he developed a special interest in the writings of James Fintan Lalor, who in 1848 had called for the revolutionary establishment of a co-operative agrarian republic. Connolly collected Lalor's writings into a pamphlet which he sent to the *Shan Van Vocht*, a nationalist journal published in Belfast which he was to use as one of his platforms for the development of his thesis concerning the inter-relationship between socialism and republican nationalism. Interestingly, the other major platform Connolly used to develop his socialist republican ideas was the English-based *Labour Leader* (then the official organ of Keir Hardie's Independent Labour

Party), though he was always to have difficulty convincing British socialists that socialism in Ireland depended upon the establishment of an Irish socialist republic independent of the authority of the British crown.

The radical nature of the socialism to which Connolly was committed has been discussed above. This is clearly articulated in what was the first formulation of his primary political goal in the context of Irish politics, the 'Establishment of AN IRISH SOCIALIST REPUBLIC based upon the public ownership by the Irish people of the land, and instruments of production, distribution and exchange'.[2] But while it is stated in this manifesto of the I.S.R.P. that 'the private ownership, by a class, of the land and instruments of production, distribution and exchange, is opposed to this vital principle of justice, and is the fundamental basis of all oppression, national, political and social', it is also, equally unambiguously, stated 'that the subjection of one nation to another, as of Ireland to the authority of the British Crown, is a barrier to the free political and economic development of the subjected nation, and can only serve the interests of the exploiting classes of both nations'.[3]

There can be little doubt, then, that right from the beginning of his involvement in Irish politics Connolly was committed to the twin goals of socialism and an independent republic. The necessity of facing the question of national independence arose primarily from the fact that at that time it dominated Irish politics, and hence failure to address the issue would have significantly marginalised the socialist movement in Ireland, if not rendered it irrelevant. This is not to say that Connolly was purely opportunistic in his approach. On the contrary, he developed a quite sophisticated theoretical analysis of the relationship between socialism and nationalism, both from a general perspective and from the perspective of the specific historical circumstances in which he was working.

II

The most fundamental element in Connolly's analysis was his insistence on a complete and unavoidable relationship of reciprocal implication between a commitment to socialism and a commitment to national independence. Connolly advanced a number of grounds for this assertion, the argument he chose to emphasise often depending on the nature of the audience he was addressing. When targeting already committed nationalists, for instance, he would begin by de-mythologising the notion of Irish freedom. If you mean by Ireland not 'the chemical elements which compose the soil of Ireland'[4] but the Irish people, then one must accept that their freedom involves both the freedom from political oppression *and* freedom from economic oppression. If one is committed to 'a full, free and happy life FOR ALL',[5] then 'nationalism without Socialism . . . is only national recreancy'.[6] He poured scorn on those who saw liberty solely in terms of political independence:

> Let us free Ireland, says the patriot who won't touch Socialism. Let us all join together and cr-r-rush the br-r-rutal Saxon. Let us all join together, says he, all classes and creeds. And, says the town worker, after we have crushed the Saxon and freed Ireland, what will we do? Oh, then you can go back to your slums, same as before. Whoop it up for liberty!
>
> And, says the agricultural worker, after we have freed Ireland, what then? Oh, then you can go scraping around for the landlord's rent or the money-lenders' interest, same as before. Whoop it up for liberty!
>
> After Ireland is free, says the patriot who won't touch Socialism, we will protect all classes, and if you won't pay your rent you will be evicted same as now. But the evicting party, under the command of the sheriff, will wear green uniforms and the Harp without the Crown, and the warrant turning you out on the roadside will be stamped with the arms of the Irish Republic. Now isn't that worth fighting for?[7]

Freedom had to include economic freedom for all, and that, for Connolly, was achievable only through socialism.

A second argument, also addressed to nationalists, was more purely economic and assumed the historical context of a capitalist world economy dominated by Britain. In such circumstances, he argued, national independence on the political level would necessarily remain merely nominal:

> If you remove the English army tomorrow and hoist the green flag over Dublin Castle, unless you set about the organisation of the Socialist Republic your efforts would be in vain.

England would still rule you. She would rule you through
her capitalists, through her landlords, through her financiers,
through the whole array of commercial and individualist institutions she has planted in this country.[8]

His claim was that real independence required economic
independence, which, given the underdeveloped state of the Irish
economy, was impossible as part of an international capitalist
order, dominated by the industrially advanced powers such as
England. It is worth noting that the validity of Connolly's
argument here depends on the doubtful feasibility of a self-
generated 'socialism in one country'.

A third approach favoured by Connolly in certain nationalist
circles was simply the polemical and *ad hominem* claim that
branded both feudal and capitalist property systems as foreign
(i.e. English) imports that were imposed on a Gaelic Ireland.
Somewhat over-romantically, Connolly viewed the pre-Norman
Gaelic clan system as an instance of primitive communism in
which the tribal lands were genuine communal property and the
clan leaders were democratically accountable to the ordinary
people.[9] By finding an historical root for socialism in Ireland,
Connolly hoped to persuade nationalists that the adoption of
socialism was implied by a deep respect for a truly Irish heritage.

Arguing that socialism ought to imply national independence,
Connolly was partly concerned to defend the pro-nationalist
reputation of socialists but also anxious to justify his commitment
to national independence to his international socialist colleagues.
At that time there was very little concern in mainstream socialist
thought with the question of national independence. To some
extent this stemmed from the fact that the question of national
independence was not in fact a live issue in the countries in which
the major socialist movements were developing, for example
England, France, Germany and the United States. In addition,
however, there was a strong 'internationalist' dimension of
socialist thought that stressed international class solidarity as the
only basis for political alliance and saw 'nationalism' as an
outdated chauvinism that would be swept aside by the developing
world economy and the international socialist movement.
Connolly's argument, however, was that there was an important
issue of democratic and, hence, socialist principle that was

completely independent of any chauvinism. In an early article, written in 1897, he drew the connection between socialism as involving common property to be organised by 'public bodies directly responsible to the entire community'[10] and the issue of the appropriate unit for the exercise of democratic popular power. His basic claim was that for a people that had been imperially oppressed the appropriate locus of popular power could not be at the imperial centre, but rather that 'representative bodies in Ireland would express more directly the will of the Irish people'.[11] World socialism would not be world government, but a free association of free peoples. At this stage of his analysis Connolly did not consider the relevance to this part of his argument of a substantial Unionist minority who wanted to maintain a political link with Britain. We shall return to this issue later.

Connolly's other grounds for relating socialism to the programme of Irish nationalism can be dealt with more briefly. Assuming the continued existence of Britain as a capitalist and imperialist power, Connolly argues, firstly, that an Ireland that was politically subject to a capitalist Britain could not possibly be socialist. The only possibility for socialism would be in an independent Ireland, and hence socialists could and should be committed to such independence.[12] Along with most other Marxists, Connolly viewed British imperialism not just as illegitimate political subjugation, but as primarily economically motivated and therefore as international capitalist exploitation. It was, consequently, a legitimate target for socialist attack. As early as 1899 Connolly was arguing, specifically in the context of the Boer War, that socialists should 'welcome the humiliation of the British arms' and anything else that would serve to destabilise capitalism in Britain.[13] Although in the earlier part of the century Connolly's desire to court nationalist favour tended to predominate in his polemic, it was these more generally anti-imperialistic positions that were to grow in significance in Connolly's public utterances, particularly after the outbreak of war in 1914.

The same was true of Connolly's final polemical argument directed specifically at radical republican nationalists which aimed to demonstrate that the only genuine and unconditional commitment to complete independence was to be found in the ranks of a working-class movement. His position here was that all classes other than the oppressed working class were primarily motivated by economic interests and would favour whatever political arrangements served those interests, no matter from what quarter, foreign or local, they arose. Hence their support of national independence was dubious and quite undependable. Furthermore, Connolly expected the Irish bourgeoisie to support a limited independence in which their capitalist interests would receive British support; as he put it in his *Shan Van Vocht* article of 1897, 'No amount of protestations should convince intelligent workers that the class that grinds them down to industrial slavery can, at the same moment, be leading them forward to national liberty.'[14] This characterisation of the nationalist motivation of the economically exploiting classes, landlords and capitalists, as being merely a means to secure their economic interests was to be one of the central themes of Connolly's *Labour in Irish History*. Whatever the validity of his arguments, there is little doubt that Connolly believed it to be the duty of socialists to strive for national independence and to oppose at all times British capitalist and imperialist power.

III

It was not only in his writings that Connolly pursued a vigorous anti-imperialist policy. In fact during the years between 1897 and 1900 his highest-profile political action consisted in various public demonstrations against such events as the celebration of Queen Victoria's Diamond Jubilee in 1897, the Boer War and the queen's visit in 1900. In many of these he collaborated with Maud Gonne, who became a personal friend. The anti-jubilee demonstration of 22 June 1897 was perhaps the most spectacular and elaborate of these occasions, and shows Connolly engaged in particularly flamboyant action. The plan was to march across the city to Parnell Square with a mock coffin draped in black and with 'British Empire' embroidered on it. Maud Gonne had made a series of black flags on which were written statistics of various social disasters, famines and evictions and so on, that had occurred during Victoria's reign. An arrangement had been made with the city lighting workers to organise a black-out, during which time Maud Gonne was to present a magic-lantern show in Parnell Square. When a police cordon prevented the procession from crossing O'Connell Bridge, Connolly rushed to the makeshift hearse, picked up the coffin and threw it into the River Liffey shouting: 'Here goes the coffin of the British Empire. To hell with the British Empire!' A general fracas ensued, with the police baton-charging the crowd and arresting Connolly. An old woman was killed in the subsequent fighting. Connolly spent the night in prison, being released on the following morning when Maud Gonne paid his fine. For Connolly this demonstration had nothing to do with chauvinistic feeling against Britain; rather, it was a clear socialist republican attack on monarchy, empire and, particularly, capitalism. A good illustration of this is the manifesto that he issued on behalf of the I.S.R.P. on the occasion of the Diamond Jubilee, this 'Feast of Flunkeyism' as he called it:

> The Irish Socialist Republican Party—which, from its inception, has never hesitated to proclaim its unswerving hostility to the British Crown, and to the political and social order of which in these islands that Crown is but the symbol—takes this opportunity of hurling at the heads of all the courtly mummers who grovel at the shrine of royalty the contempt and hatred of the Irish Revolutionary Democracy . . . The working class alone have nothing to hope for save in a revolutionary reconstruction of society.[15]

The anti-jubilee demonstration was only the first of many that Connolly was to organise. Protesting at Queen Victoria's visit in 1900, Connolly was again arrested, this time in the company of Maud Gonne, after he had broken through a police cordon, charging at it with a horse and cart. They were released without charge on that occasion.

Connolly's day-to-day political activity continued with the usual round of socialist agitation. A major new departure occurred in 1898 when, with a loan of £50 from Keir Hardie and some advance subscriptions from Scottish colleagues, he launched the first edition of a weekly socialist newspaper, the *Workers' Republic*. For the next few years the *Workers' Republic* was to serve as Connolly's major platform for the dissemination of his radical socialist analysis of Irish political affairs. Commenting routinely on the events of the day, Connolly also contributed more extensive pieces in which he addressed more general issues,

such as the Irish language movement, the socialist attitude to
political violence, and so on. The *Workers' Republic* was the first of
several such papers Connolly was to edit and write for volumin-
ously in the coming years. It did well initially, selling for a penny a
copy, mostly at his outdoor meetings. After twelve issues, however,
it closed down; but he relaunched it in the following year after he
had purchased a small press. He set and printed the paper
himself at the party's offices in Middle Abbey Street. Incidentally,
that particular press was smashed by police when they ransacked
the offices on the night of the demonstration against Queen
Victoria's visit referred to above. Whatever else Connolly had
achieved, he had gained a certain notoriety with the Dublin
police.

During those first years in Dublin the economic circumstances
of Connolly and his family were more often than not desperate.
For long periods his salary of £1 a week, which was little enough
to begin with, was not paid at all. They lived in slum conditions in
a one-roomed flat in a tenement building in Charlemont Street,
and later in Pimlico in the Coombe area of Dublin. There is a
harrowing account in his daughter Nora's memoir of an evening
when her father returned from a labouring job that he had just
secured; he collapsed into a chair and broke down in tears, partly
as a result of sheer exhaustion, but also because of his shame at
what he thought was his physical inability to do the job he had just
got. In the end, without comment, his wife Lillie sold the very last
of her jewellery to buy food so that he would have the strength to
work.

Through this work Connolly became directly involved in the
trade union movement in Dublin. In 1901 he was elected by the
United Labourers' Union to the Dublin Trades Council, an
organisation of representatives of Dublin trade unions. He was
characteristically active in the Trades Councils, instigating
proposals to press the city authorities to address the notorious
problem of Dublin's tenement slums. He stood, unsuccessfully, in
local elections for the Wood Quay ward; at this time he was
subjected to a particularly vicious campaign of vilification, being
branded from the Catholic pulpits as an atheist and an enemy of
Christianity. In the circumstances, it is not surprising that out of a
total of 1,875 votes cast, Connolly received only 431.

From 1902 on, however, Connolly began to emerge as an almost full-time socialist speaker and organiser. A paid speaking tour of Scotland and England was arranged for him, and he spent much of the year travelling up and down these countries lecturing to various labour and socialist groups and engaging in the usual street-corner propaganda. As his reputation in socialist circles became consolidated, a socialist lecture tour of the United States was organised under the auspices of the radical Socialist Labor Party, led by Daniel De Leon. It was hoped that Connolly might be effective in generating support for the party among Irish-Americans. He left for the United States in August 1902 for a gruelling four-month tour during which he was constantly on the move; each day he travelled from one town to the next, and each night he lectured on various aspects of socialism. One of Connolly's aims was to increase the circulation of his *Workers' Republic* in America, soliciting subscriptions and sending them back to Dublin. It was precisely this that led within months to Connolly's split with the I.S.R.P.

There is evidence that during his prolonged absences from Dublin in 1902 Connolly was becoming somewhat disenchanted with the level of commitment and dedication that his Dublin colleagues were prepared to give to the party. He complained in letters about late publication of the paper, and lackadaisical attitudes to accountancy and correspondence. One development which particularly disturbed him was the use of the party offices as an illegal drinking club. Connolly himself was a teetotaller, but was also concerned that the activities of the club might attract the adverse attention of the authorities and be used by them as a pretext for suppressing the party. Eventually mismanagement of the club's accounts brought about a total fiasco in the financial affairs of the I.S.R.P. that was to lead to Connolly's resignation. Basically, the advanced subscriptions for the *Workers' Republic* that Connolly was so painstakingly collecting were being spent in Dublin in subsidising the badly run drinking club. When, on his return, he discovered that the money he had sent from America had disappeared and that the party could not afford to pay the instalments on its printing-press, he resigned as party organiser. This occurred in February 1903. Following on an even worse defeat than previously in local elections held in January—this time he received only 243 votes—Connolly began to sever his links with the I.S.R.P.

A speaking tour in Scotland was organised for him in May, and while there he took on for three months the job of national organiser for the Socialist Labour Party in Edinburgh, which had broken away from the Social Democratic Federation. He had already decided, however, on emigration with his family to the United States. He left on his own for America in September 1903. As with so many other immigrants, his plan was to secure employment, save money and send for his family when he could afford to. He left his wife and family, now consisting of five children, Mona, Nora, Aideen, Ina and Roddy, in Dublin. It would be nearly a year until, in tragic circumstances that will be later recounted, he was to be reunited with his family in New York. It is also significant that none of his Dublin socialist colleagues went to bid him farewell.

3

AMERICA AND INDUSTRIAL UNIONISM, 1903–10

I

Connolly's original intention on arriving in New York was to secure work in the printing business, specifically with the firm that printed the Socialist Labor Party newspapers. Encountering difficulties in getting a union card, without which he could not get a printing job, he changed his plans and went to stay with his cousins, Margaret and Thomas Humes, who lived up the Hudson in the city of Troy. There he got a job with the Metropolitan Life Insurance Company as a door-to-door insurance collector. He had, of course, many contacts and acquaintances, particularly in the Socialist Labor Party, of which he now became an official member. He soon became active in the affairs of the party, attending meetings and receiving invitations to speak and lecture.

Unlike the Socialist Party of America, which under the leadership of Eugene Debs was to be a broadly based and largely reformist party, the Socialist Labor Party (S.L.P.) was a Marxist revolutionary party affiliated with the Second International. At the time of Connolly's arrival in New York the S.L.P. was a vibrant organisation comprising several thousand members, publishing a daily, weekly and monthly journal. Its leader, Daniel De Leon, was an extraordinary and charismatic figure. Dedicated, flamboyant and brilliant, he had a definite authoritarian strain which brooked no opposition, and Connolly was soon to fall foul of the great man when he was led to challenge certain 'orthodox' beliefs of the S.L.P. that had De Leon's imprimatur.

At a meeting of the party, for example, Connolly discovered to his astonishment that there was a general uncritical belief among S.L.P. members in what was known as the 'Iron Law of Wages', in accordance with the preferred views of the leader. Connolly was led to open a debate in the party on this and other issues, in particular on the relation between a commitment to socialism and the holding of certain religious and moral beliefs. In a letter to the S.L.P.'s *Weekly People* in March 1904 he dealt with these matters. Connolly's intervention initiated a controversy with the party leader, De Leon, that was eventually to result in a rancorous personal and political split between the two men in which, not surprisingly, De Leon prevailed. De Leon suceeded in getting the S.L.P. to issue an official censure against the impertinent newcomer; but though chastened, Connolly remained an active member of the party for years to come.[1]

The dispute over the law of wages, though more technically interesting, was of lesser significance. The 'Iron Law of Wages' is associated in the socialist tradition with Ferdinand Lassalle. It claimed, simply, that workers in a capitalist economy could not gain a rise in real wages, since every nominal increase was bound to be offset by an exactly corresponding increase in prices. Connolly argued that Marx had himself rejected this thesis, and also that it was actually false. In this case there seems little doubt in retrospect that Connolly was perfectly correct on both counts.[2]

The more fundamental dispute between Connolly and De Leon arose over the question of the relationship between socialism and religious and moral beliefs, and specifically the acceptance of the conventional morality of monogamous marriage. This is a more complex question, more central to Connolly's thought, and requires further consideration.[3] Put simply, Connolly believed that certain religious beliefs were perfectly compatible with a genuine commitment to socialism as an economic and political system; in addition, if religious beliefs included a strong egalitarian and humanitarian moral dimension they could themselves ground a socialistic commitment. Furthermore, Connolly believed that it was a self-defeating policy to refuse to co-operate in practice with or to alienate those who held beliefs with which one might not agree simply because they were not logically consistent with a socialistic commitment. The only criteria for practical co-operation should be the authenticity of a person's aspiration to socialism.

Even if we accept this part of Connolly's argument, however, his position on religion and the acceptance of the conventional morality of monogamous marriage might seem more difficult to reconcile with his endorsement of Marxist historical materialism. Historical materialism purports to explain the emergence and persistence of such things as religious belief, forms of marriage and their associated moralities in terms of how they serve the preservation of exploitative property relations. Surely such a theory impugns the validity of religious belief and the supposed intrinsic worth of monogamous marriage. It is now accepted that Connolly, for most of his adult life, had completely abandoned his Christian Catholic beliefs. In the now well-known letter to his friend Matheson written in 1908 he asserted: 'For myself, though I have usually posed as a Catholic, I have not gone to my duty for 15 years, and have not the slightest tincture of faith left.'[4] However, although he trenchantly attacked religious authorities for their explicit political involvement,[5] he never attacked religious belief as such, and he explicitly claimed that monogamous marriage was an intrinsically valuable part of civilisation which would not be destroyed and replaced by historical development, but perfected and completed.[6] Connolly did, in fact, have a perfectly intelligible defence of his position that can be seen as being based on the fundamental principle that an explanation of the origin of a belief or social institution does not in itself have any logically necessary implications for the truth of the belief or the continuing value of the institution. He illustrated this by citing the example of the technology that had been developed by capitalism and was used to generate capitalist profit, but had a value for human beings as such, and so could and should be preserved and perfected in a future socialist society.[7] It is no doubt true that Connolly's position on religion, marriage and conventional morality generally were much more conservative than those of Marx and other Marxists. His main and overriding priority, however, was the achievement of socialism and the ending of what he saw as capitalist economic oppression, and he was prepared to co-operate with those who shared the same political commitment irrespective of their other beliefs, the debate concerning which he saw as a distraction from the main task in hand.

II

Meanwhile Connolly had settled into his job as an insurance salesman and by August 1904 had saved enough money to pay for the fare for his family to join him. Sadly, on the very day before they were due to leave Dublin, Connolly's eldest daughter, Mona, using her apron to lift a pot of hot water from the fire accidentally set herself on fire and was so badly burned that she later died. Friends of the family advised Lillie to go ahead with her plans as soon as a deferred sailing could be arranged. Connolly, however, had already left Troy to meet his family in New York and could not be contacted. When they did not arrive on the appointed sailing, Connolly met ship after ship, becoming more and more puzzled and worried, only to be utterly devastated when, a week later, they finally did arrive and he was informed of the tragic news.

The family settled down in what for them was the unaccustomed luxury of a house of their own in Troy. Trouble, though, was not long in returning. Connolly lost his job with Metropolitan Life, and when he could not find alternative employment in Troy, he moved temporarily to New York, where he stayed with an old I.S.R.P. colleague, Jack Mulray, working at whatever bits and pieces of temporary jobs he could pick up. He returned to his family in Troy in 1905 to work for another insurance firm, but the job proved unprofitable, and he eventually found work as a machinist in the Singer Sewing Machine Company in Newark. The family moved there in the autumn of 1905. Connolly had had no experience in the work, but he passed himself off as a skilled machinist and was apparently successful in teaching himself the basic skills. He was to continue working for the company for over a year, earning what was about the average industrial wage at the time of $15 per week.

Connolly remained active in the S.L.P., eventually becoming a member of the national executive, but on the political front the most significant development for him was the foundation in 1905, under the leadership of 'Big Bill' Haywood, of the Industrial Workers of the World. The period during which Connolly was in America was one in which economic recession generated a significant level of industrial unrest, leading to the formation of numerous militant and radical labour and socialist organisations with relatively widespread popular support. The leader of the Socialist Party of America, Eugene Debs, for example, secured over a million votes in the 1908 presidential election, though it should be noted that the S.P.A. was relatively moderate in its politics. The I.W.W., on the other hand, was an 'industrial union' adopting militant tactics and the ideology of revolutionary syndicalism or 'industrial unionism'. Connolly joined the I.W.W. soon after its foundation and was to become both an active and important member and an eloquent spokesman for its ideology, particularly in his pamphlet *Socialism Made Easy*, published in 1908, which sold very well in America, Ireland, England and even Australia.

III

The syndicalist ideology—or, as Connolly himself preferred to call it, 'industrial unionism'—had both a trade union and a socialist revolutionary strategy dimension. On the trade union side, industrial unionism was a systematisation of the ideas motivating the 'new unionism' that began to emerge towards the end of the nineteenth century.[8] Initially the trade union movement had been characterised by craft unions. As their name implies, such unions restricted membership to those who, often after long apprenticeship, had acquired one of the numerous traditional crafts, such as mason, cabinet-maker, etc. Craft unions tended to be moderate, conservative organisations that charged relatively high subscription rates and operated largely as friendly societies, providing insurance benefits in times of injury and sickness. They also tended to pursue an 'acceptable' standard of remuneration for their members by, as Emmet O'Connor puts it, 'maintaining demand for labour through control of apprenticeships'.[9]

The 'new unions', in contrast, went for mass membership, targeted general 'unskilled' labour, charged low subscription rates, and adopted the militant tactics of strike action to gain an increase in wages or improvement of working conditions. New unionism tended to endorse what was seen as 'extreme' action, such as the blacking of goods and the sympathetic strike undertaken by workers who might not be directly involved in a particular dispute. This was to be facilitated, particularly in the explicit ideology of industrial unionism, by creating for all workers 'One Big Union', this being subdivided not by craft or type of occupation, but by the industry in which people worked. The purpose of this was to enable united and concerted action within a particular industrial plant or branch of industry and, if necessary, to call on the support of other members of the same union in related branches of industry either in the form of the blacking of tainted goods or through the sympathetic strike. In 'Industrialism and the Trade Unions' Connolly describes the ludicrousness of the situation in which the carpenters in a particular city in dispute with their bosses must appeal to their headquarters and

> general membership, from San Francisco to Rhode Island, and from Podunk to Kalamazoo . . . but while they are soliciting and receiving the support of their fellow-carpenters they are precluded from calling out in sympathy with them the painters who follow them in their work, the plumbers whose pipes they cover up, the steamfitters who work at their elbows, or the plasterer who precedes them. Yet the co-operation of these workers with them in their strikes is a thousandfold more important than the voting of strike funds which would keep them out on strike.[10]

Such a union would, for Connolly, prove a near invincible weapon in the day-to-day struggle of workers with their bosses. The old-style craft unions were, according to Connolly, 'tied hand and foot, handcuffed and hobbled'.[11]

Important as the trade union dimension was, it was only secondary to the part that industrial unionism would play as in the central strategy of a socialist revolution. This strategy, for Connolly, had two aspects. The first consisted in the building up of a working-class organisation 'capable of the revolutionary act of taking over society'.[12] The necessity for such an organisation arose because although Connolly welcomed 'the abandonment of the unfortunate insurrectionism of the early Socialists' and its replacement by the 'the slower, but surer method of the ballot-box',[13] he anticipated, along with the other socialists, that 'the ballot will yet be stricken from the hands of the socialist party'.[14] It was, then, a serious question for revolutionary socialists as to what, in those circumstances, the appropriate response should be. In 'Ballots, Bullets, or — ?'[15] while not, in principle, rejecting the bullet, Connolly claimed:

> We still have the opportunity to forge a weapon capable of winning the fight for us against political usurpation and all the military powers of earth, sea or air. That weapon is to be forged in the furnace of the struggle in the workshop, mine, factory or railroad, and its name is industrial unionism.[16]

The industrial union, uniting the working class in a single organisation, provided the means whereby that working class could assert its democratic power over the affairs of society. European continental syndicalism usually identified the method of such revolutionary takeover as the 'general strike'.

The second aspect of this revolutionary strategy is even more important. As early as 1901, in the first section of *The New Evangel*, Connolly had argued that state ownership is not, in itself, socialism. 'To the cry of the middle-class reformers, "make this or that the property of the government", we reply "yes, in proportion as the workers are ready to make the government their property".'[17] After encountering and developing the ideas of industrial unionism, Connolly could argue that 'This conception of Socialism destroys at one blow all the fears of a bureaucratic State, ruling and ordering the lives of every individual from above.'[18] The basic idea was that an omnicompetent centralised state was inappropriate for the economic decision-making of a future socialist society. Such decision-making should be radically decentralised following the functional divisions of industrial production and distribution. The organisation of the one big industrial union along the same functional division lines

> prepares within the framework of capitalist society the working forms of the Socialist republic, and thus, while increasing the resisting power of the worker against present encroachments of the capitalist class, it familiarizes him with the idea that the union he is helping to build up is destined to supplant that class in the control of the industry in which he is employed.[19]

This was a grandiose ideal with the power, as Connolly put it, 'to transform the dry detail work of trade union organisation into the constructive work of revolutionary Socialism'.[20]

During his remaining years in America, Connolly was to become more and more involved in the affairs of the I.W.W. It is not surprising to learn that his militancy within the union eventually led to difficulties with his employers in the Singer Sewing Machine Company, and by 1907 he was again jobless. Eventually, however, he obtained work as an I.W.W. organiser, though his weekly salary of $18 was often not forthcoming. However, he approached his work with characteristic energy and was successful in recruiting many workers into the union. In addition, as the New York correspondent for the I.W.W. paper he became known throughout the organisation.

All of this coincided with his split with De Leon and the S.L.P. As mentioned above, by 1907 Connolly had been elected to the national executive of the S.L.P. Early in that year, however, what started as a seemingly trivial disagreement between Connolly and De Leon on certain organisational matters led De Leon once again to seek major party condemnation of Connolly. Old animosities surfaced, and eventually De Leon denounced Connolly as a *agent provocateur* —as a Jesuit spy, in fact. In the face of such rancour and opposition, Connolly let his membership of the party lapse and gradually severed all links. In retrospect he came to view De Leon as something of an autocrat and an impostor who only wanted a party staffed by sycophantic followers. By 1908 he had joined the reformist and compromising Socialist Party of America, because he 'felt it better to be one of the revolutionary minority inside the party than a mere discontented grumbler out of political life entirely'.[21] In the following year he was appointed as one of the six national organisers of the party at a salary of $21 a week. Given that his salary was paid regularly and that he received travelling expenses and could market his pamphlets, Connolly finally attained a reasonable level of economic security in America.

Despite this level of involvement in trade union and S.P.A. affairs, from 1907 on Connolly began to think seriously about a return to Ireland. In March 1907 he had formed in New York the Irish Socialist Federation (I.S.F.). Connolly had always believed that the natural affinity between members of any ethnic immigrant group could form the basis of both trade union and socialist organisation. Thus, along with some fellow-emigrants from Ireland, notably Jack Mulray, and with the help of some Irish-American radicals such as Elizabeth Gurley, he founded the I.S.F. specifically to foster revolutionary consciousness among the Irish working class in America.

Yet while the I.S.F. was directed specifically at the Irish in America, it was nevertheless to be the proximate cause of Connolly's re-establishing contact with some of his socialist colleagues back in Ireland. In particular, he contacted William

O'Brien, who had been a member of the now defunct I.S.R.P. Some of the members of that party had regrouped as the Socialist Party of Ireland, with offices at 35 Parliament Street, Dublin. Soon Connolly was in frequent contact with O'Brien. By 1908 the possibility was being aired of getting Connolly to return to Ireland as the official organiser of the Socialist Party of Ireland. Initially he insisted that he would return only if the whole family returned together and he could be assured of a properly organised job with a salary that would provide a decent standard of living for his family. As there seemed to be little likelihood of this, he began to consider alternatives.

In 1908, as the mouthpiece of the Irish Socialist Federation, Connolly had established the journal *The Harp*. Partly in anticipation of returning to Ireland, and partly because he thought *The Harp* could be produced more cheaply in Ireland, he transferred the paper to Dublin in late 1909. Meanwhile he was still engaged in extensive travelling all over the United States, lecturing and organising for the Socialist Party of America. By 1910, however, he had decided to accept the offer of an 'exploratory' tour of Ireland, Scotland and England, to be financed as usual by a series of speaking engagements. When James Larkin, whom he did not know personally at the time, wrote offering his services in organising the tour, he finally decided to accept. He arrived back in Ireland on 26 July 1910.

James Larkin, from an Irish working-class background in Liverpool, had arrived in Belfast as union organiser for the British-based National Union of Dock Labourers (N.U.D.L.). Larkin was a militant firebrand whose revolutionary stance and uncompromising action eventually led the British leaders of the N.U.D.L. to dismiss him from his job late in 1908. He responded by forming the Irish Transport and General Workers' Union. At the instigation of the leaders of the N.U.D.L., Larkin had been charged with the mismanagement of union funds, been found guilty and sentenced to twelve months in prison. When Connolly arrived in Dublin, Larkin was in Mountjoy Jail, just beginning his sentence, though a strong 'Larkin Release' movement was started in which Connolly was active. In addition, Connolly began the schedule of lectures and speeches, first around Ireland and then Scotland and England. Negotiations with O'Brien and the

Start w/ Larkin

Able to identify w/ worker, know their plight

Socialist Party of Ireland continued concerning the possibility of raising enough money for Connolly and his family to return to Ireland. Since it appeared that sufficient funds would not be available, Connolly decided to return to America. However, Larkin was released after serving only three months of his sentence and threw his weight behind the organisation of an appeal fund to finance Connolly's appointment as national organiser for the S.P.I. Sufficient money was raised to bring the family over, and the end of 1910 saw Connolly and his family resettled in Ireland, this time for good.

4

IRELAND, 1910–14: THE IRISH TRANSPORT AND GENERAL WORKERS' UNION AND THE 1913 LOCK-OUT

I

Within a few months of his return to Dublin, Connolly succeeded in publishing one of his most substantial works, *Labour in Irish History*, a book-length study of certain aspects of Irish history from what Connolly himself identified as a Marxist perspective: 'that in every historical epoch the prevailing method of economic production and exchange, and the social organisation necessarily following from it, forms the basis upon which alone can be explained the political and intellectual history of that epoch'.[1]

The book had been long in gestation. From his first arrival in Ireland in 1896 Connolly had appreciated the importance of developing a radical, socialist-based interpretation of Irish history. During periods of unemployment he had undertaken research in the National Library in Dublin, concentrating his inquiries particularly on the period of the Famine and immersing himself in the writings of the nineteenth-century agrarian radical James Fintan Lalor. In *Labour and Irish History* Connolly set out, on the one hand, to debunk what he considered to be certain myths in the history of Irish nationalism. As we saw in Chapter 2 when analysing Connolly's general theory concerning the relationship between socialism and nationalism, it was his fixed belief that the economically privileged classes were always primarily concerned with protecting their own economic interests and, whether consciously or otherwise, would adopt whatever political stance best served those economic interests. Ranging from the close of the Williamite war in 1691 to the end of the nineteenth century, he attempted to illustrate in detail the effects of economic structures and interests on the political history of Ireland. In particular, he set out to show that much of the history of Irish nationalism was not to be explained by a patriotic love of Ireland: the patriotism of the Jacobites, for example, he claimed, 'consisted in an effort to retain for themselves the lands of the native peasantry; the English influence against which they protested was the influence of their fellow-thieves in England, hungry for a share of the spoil'.[2] Invariably the upper classes, whether landlords, merchants or capitalists, put their own economic interests first. On the other hand, the work sets out to show that there was a continuous radical tradition in Ireland. Beginning with 'the Gaelic principle of common ownership',[3] Connolly searches for evidence of what he considers to be the genuine egalitarian radicalism of 'the militant Irish democracy' from the actions of peasant organisations such as the Oakboys and the Hearts of Steel to the theoretical anticipation of republicanism in the United Irishmen, and of socialism in the works of William Thompson and the co-operative experiment of Ralahine in the nineteenth century. The book demonstrates that Connolly had a very wide knowledge of Irish social, economic and political history, and it draws on an impressive range of documentary sources. And while even the Soviet historian Artemy Kolpakov, who wrote an introduction to a Russian translation of Connolly's work, chides him somewhat with 'a purely economic explanation of historical events, against which Engels in his time warned',[4] it cannot be denied that *Labour in Irish History* provides a refreshingly iconoclastic attack on some of the 'great men' of Irish history, written with passion and vigour.

Of particular interest in the book is Connolly's acknowledgement of the work of the Cork-born economic and political theorist, William Thompson, whose *Inquiry into the Principles of the Distribution of Wealth* (1824) significantly anticipated the critical analysis of capitalism later developed by Marx. Of note also is the chapter entitled 'An Irish Utopia' in which Connolly provides a fascinating account of the socialist experiment at Ralahine, County Clare, in the 1830s.[5] Altogether the whole work is a testimony of Connolly's belief that the victims of economic and political oppression can overcome whatever forces may temporarily divide them and unite to secure their collective liberation. As he put it, referring specifically to religious divides in Ireland, in the very last lines of the book,

The pressure of a common exploitation can make enthusiastic rebels out of a Protestant working class, earnest champions of civil and religious liberty out of Catholics, and out of both a united social democracy.[6]

At about the same time as he completed *Labour in Irish History* Connolly also published a second, shorter and more polemical tract. *Labour, Nationality and Religion* is more of a reactive work, consisting as it does of a detailed rebuttal of the charges made against socialism and socialists by Father Kane, S.J., in a series of Lenten lectures given earlier in 1910 while Connolly was still in America. The pamphlet, a substantial seventy pages long, begins with the important point that the essence of Catholic belief is not to be confused with any and every stance taken up by church authorities. Connolly gleefully proceeds to document a whole series of political meddlings by representatives of the church which, in retrospect, were to be generally condemned as wrongheaded, self-serving compromises with whoever happened to be politically and economically important at the time.[7] He was attempting to set as a baseline his polemically important point that the church authorities are not necessarily right, especially when they get involved in political and economic and social affairs. The body of the text consists of a detailed analysis of Father Kane's arguments against socialism. It is, on the one hand, an attempt to defend the essential principles of socialism, such as the illegitimacy of capitalist profit; on the other hand, it constitutes Connolly's most extensive discussion of the issue of socialism and religion, distinguishing between a genuine commitment to socialism, which, he argued, was compatible with genuine Catholic morality, and various other beliefs and theories that some socialists (and non-socialists) have held. On this central issue Connolly is both acute and sparklingly polemical. For example, against the charge that a socialist society would be populated by 'beasts of immorality' and 'free-thinkers' he retorts:

> Sufficient to remind our readers that, even according to the oft-repeated assertion of Father Kane, Socialism means a state of society in which the will of the people should be supreme, that therefore Marx and Bebel and Liebknecht and Vandervelde and Blatchford were not and are not working for the establishment of a system in which they would be able to

force their theories about religion upon the people, but for a system in which the people would be free to accept only that of which their conscience approved.[8]

II

In the meantime Connolly and his family had settled in a house in the Ballsbridge area of Dublin and Connolly himself turned his attention to the affairs of the Socialist Party of Ireland and to political matters generally. He immediately began to build up the party, organising the usual recruiting and propaganda meetings and founding new branches outside the Dublin area. It was also at this time that he initiated moves to found a united political party in Ireland that would be able to contest elections in a future Home Rule parliament. On a more bread-and-butter issue (literally) he approached the Irish Women's Franchise League and Maud Gonne's Daughters of Erin with a plan to organise a campaign to put pressure on the Irish authorities to extend to Ireland the implementation of new legislation in England that provided for the feeding of needy children in schools. We have mentioned his previous co-operation with Maud Gonne back in the 1890s, and it is worth adding at this point that these were only a few instances of a long history of collaboration with women's movements. Connolly had rather conventional attitudes to monogamy and marital morality; but he had an absolutely consistent record of co-operation with the militant feminist movements of the time and held steadfastly to his support for women's political rights. Furthermore, he demonstrated in his writings great sympathy and insight into the particular plight of the working woman who becomes through her 'double domestic toil . . . the slave of the domestic needs of her family' in addition to being driven out to work in which she is 'overworked and underpaid'.[9]

Despite Connolly's recruiting efforts, the Socialist Party of Ireland was simply not large enough to be able to finance a permanent organiser, and his salary was often not paid. For reasons which are not entirely clear, he moved with his family from Dublin to a house off the Falls Road in Belfast some time in 1911. And it was then that he found permanent employment as a full-time organiser of the militant new union, the Irish Transport and General Workers' Union (I.T.G.W.U.) founded by James Larkin in 1909, which was now in a position to finance a full-time official in Belfast. Connolly had now found a permanent settled position in the Irish labour movement, but though he continued to work for the I.T.G.W.U. for the rest of his life, his time thereafter was to be divided between his trade union work, his renewed efforts to form an Irish Labour Party as the basis of a united socialist movement, and his always extensive writing.

The trade union movement in Ireland, as elsewhere, had been characterised mainly by craft unions, with general unskilled labourers poorly organised. It was precisely such labourers, dockers, carters, builders' labourers, transport workers, etc., that Larkin's union was aimed at. Arriving in Ireland in 1907 as the representative of the British-based National Union of Dock Labourers, Larkin, on his dismissal for militancy, founded his own independent union, the I.T.G.W.U., in 1909. By 1913 it was becoming a powerful organisation, with upwards of 14,000 members, a weekly newspaper, the *Irish Worker*, and offices at Liberty Hall, Beresford Place, in the centre of Dublin. By all accounts, 'Big Jim' Larkin was a revolutionary firebrand, capable of powerful emotive oratory and given to extremely militant rhetoric. Like Connolly, he made no secret of his implacable opposition to capitalism and his espousal of the tactics of lightning strikes and sympathetic action. Among many of Dublin's 'respectable' classes Larkin and his union were seen as dangerous revolutionaries hell-bent on destroying modern civilisation.

As a full-time official of the I.T.G.W.U., Connolly too quickly acquired a reputation not only as an efficient organiser and administrator and a tireless fighter for the interests of his members, but also as a skilled negotiator who could be trusted by all sides. The events surrounding a bitter labour dispute that occurred in 1911–12 in Wexford illustrate the latter. The problems began when workers in three iron foundries were dismissed for joining the Transport Union. This was followed by a strike by the dock workers; scab labour was brought in by the employers, protests were organised, and a Transport Union man, P. T. Daly, was arrested and imprisoned. In January 1912 Connolly was sent for. Within days he had drawn up compromise proposals which were accepted by all sides and the dispute was settled. He then successfully campaigned for Daly's release. He stayed for a couple of months organising a new Foundrymen's Union, which had been part of his settlement plan, before returning to Belfast.

Connolly's trade union involvement was still seen by him in the context of his syndicalism or industrial unionism. However, unlike some European syndicalists, he never renounced the necessity for political organisation. The foundation of a trade-union-based Irish socialist party that would bid for electoral success to represent the interests of labour was one of Connolly's major ambitions. At the meeting of the Irish Trades Union Congress in 1911 he succeeded in getting accepted a resolution which committed the congress to the establishment of an Irish Labour Party. Although it was some time until the resolution was implemented in practice, Connolly's action is seen as the founding moment of the Irish Labour Party.

Connolly returned to political writing at this time, and the fruit of his thought was made evident, particularly in the set of papers eventually published in 1915 as *The Reconquest of Ireland*. In this book Connolly returned to his old subject, the relationship between nationalism and socialism, emphasising as he had always done, that the reconquest of Ireland, leading to Irish freedom, had to be primarily economic: 'The principle of public ownership brings us nearer to the reconquest of Ireland by its people; it means the gradual resumption of the common ownership of all Ireland by all the Irish.'[10] However, living as he was in Belfast at the time, Connolly could not fail to be aware that these words 'all Ireland by all the Irish' were far from unambiguous in their political implications. Under the leadership of Sir Edward Carson, loyalist Unionist opposition to Home Rule, particularly as including Ulster, was growing more militant. The year 1912 witnessed outbreaks of extreme sectarian tension among the Belfast working class, one of the worst instances being the forcible expulsion of 2,000 Catholics from their jobs in Harland & Wolff shipyards by Protestant workers. Even 400 English and Scottish workers were forced out for refusing to co-operate with the militant Protestants. Within the labour and socialist movement itself, Connolly had encountered opposition to a united independent Ireland.

Connolly's position on Irish independence in the light of significant loyalist opposition is clear and unambiguous.[11] On the most abstract level, Connolly regarded modern nation-states as expressions of 'the coercive forces of capitalist society', having grown 'out of . . . territorial divisions of power in the hands of the ruling class in past ages'.[12] However, he accepted that for administrative purposes the functional decentralisation of a syndicalist society required 'territorial' organisation. The appropriate unit for that organisation would definitely not be that defined by the results of imperial and colonial domination. To Connolly, only someone blinded by bigotry could fail to see that the appropriate administrative unit for dealing with Irish affairs was Ireland and had as little to do with England and the British Empire as it had to do with China or Timbuctoo:

> The Socialist Party of Ireland recognises and most enthusiastically endorses the principle of internationalism, but it realises that that principle must be sought through the medium of universal brotherhood rather than by the self-extinction of distinct nations within the political maw of overgrown Empires.[13]

But what are the implications of this principle if within this 'distinct nation' there is a numerically very significant group with deep-rooted aspirations for continued unity with Britain? Again, Connolly's position on such aspirations is clear and uncompromising.

Firstly, Connolly argued that, as adopted by the upper classes, Unionism was an ideology whose purpose was to serve 'the interests of the oppressive property rights of rackrenting landlords and sweating capitalists'[14] and hence, from the perspective of radical socialism, had no legitimacy. It was, anyway, 'an atavistic survival of a dark and ignorant past'.[15] As accepted by the Protestant working class, it was, in Connolly's view, a clear case of duped false-consciousness:

> If the North-East corner of Ireland is, therefore, the home of a people whose minds are saturated with conceptions of political activity fit only for the atmosphere of the seventeenth century, if the sublime ideas of an all-embracing democracy equally as insistent upon its duties as upon its rights have as yet found poor lodgment here, the fault lies not with this

generation of toilers, but with those pastors and masters who deceived it and enslaved it in the past—and deceived it in order that they might enslave it.[16]

Secondly, even from a democratic perspective, loyalist aspiration should not, for Connolly, be acceded to; numerically significant as support for loyalism was, it was a clearly in a minority. It has to be said that nowadays some democratic theorists[17] would argue that democracy does not imply aggressive majoritarianism, but rather that the political equality of democracy requires giving to minorities as well as majorities a definite input into the determination of political outcomes. The issues of loyalism and northern sectarianism were, however, soon to be relegated to the sideline by the fierce labour struggle that erupted in Dublin in 1913.

III

The '1913 lock-out', in which Connolly was to play a major role, was in fact a series of lock-outs, strikes and counter-lockouts that rapidly brought Dublin to the brink of industrial civil war. The background can be briefly sketched.[18] The living conditions of the working-class poor of Dublin in the first decade of the century were dire in the extreme. About 80,000 people lived in run-down tenement accommodation, many families living crowded into a single room. According to official statistics, over 20,000 people lived in 'third-class housing', defined as literally unfit for human habitation. Disease associated with malnutrition was rife, and levels of infant mortality were appalling. Unemployment was high, and even those who could find work were badly treated. Many thousands of men and women worked as unskilled labourers, men being paid about £1 a week, women rarely over 12s. The average income was barely able to provide a subsistence diet of tea, bread, dripping and potatoes, supplemented sometimes by a modicum of bacon and fish. Work, of course, was long and arduous, the average working week being about sixty hours.

It was against this background that Larkin's I.T.G.W.U. began to develop an ever more confrontational stance. Foremost among Larkin's opponents in Dublin was William Martin Murphy, who by

1913 had become a central figure in the commercial life of Dublin; he was a major shareholder in and chairman of the board of the Dublin United Tramways Company, as well as owning the grandiose Imperial Hotel in O'Connell Street and the *Irish Independent* newspaper. He was a leading light of the Dublin Chamber of Commerce and the instigator in the formation of the Employers' Federation, organised to provide a united front on the employers' side against 'Larkinism' in the trade union movement. According to William O'Brien, writing to Connolly in 1911,

> 'Smash Larkin' is the battle cry in Dublin just now. All the papers—but in particular the *Independent*—are going for him bald-headed. The meeting of the Dublin Chamber of Commerce yesterday, and the decision to form an organisation of Irish Employers, shows a determination to down the Transport Union at all costs.[19]

Matters came to a head when in August 1913 Murphy and the directors of the Tramways Company dismissed a hundred men from the company for their alleged membership of the I.T.G.W.U. and issued a 'pledge' which all workers in Murphy's companies were required to sign on pain of dismissal. The pledge was a direct assault on the union; it read:

> I hereby undertake to carry out all instructions given me by or on behalf of my employers, and further, I agree to immediately resign my membership of the Irish Transport and General Workers' Union (if a member) and I further undertake that I will not join or in any way support this union.[20]

Larkin responded by calling a strike of the tramway workers on 26 August. Immediately street fighting broke out between strikers, 'scabs' and police. On the evening of the first day of the strike Larkin addressed a meeting in Beresford Place; using fiery revolutionary language, he urged the strikers to defend themselves and called for a mass meeting in O'Connell Street for the following Sunday. Two days later Larkin and several of his colleagues were arrested and charged with conspiracy and incitement. At this point an urgent telegram summoned Connolly from Belfast to help with the organisation of the strike.

Larkin — there for start

Along with Larkin, who had been released on bail, Connolly addressed another meeting in Beresford Place on the Friday evening. Larkin went into hiding, but Connolly and William Partridge were arrested and summarily tried. Connolly was defiant, refused to give bail, and was imprisoned in Mountjoy. Major street violence erupted in the following days. On Saturday evening a demonstration of striking workers was baton-charged by the police, resulting in the deaths of two young men, James Nolan and James Byrne. The Sunday meeting in O'Connell Street had been banned by the authorities, but, despite a heavy police presence, Larkin kept his promise to attend. Disguised as an old man with a beard and dressed in a frock-coat, he succeeded in gaining access to—of all places—the Imperial Hotel and proceeded to address the people in the street from an upstairs window. He was immediately arrested, and in what the *Freeman's Journal* of Monday 1 September described as 'Appalling Scenes in City' the police baton-charged the crowd, injuring many hundreds of people, most of whom were thought, in fact, to be innocent bystanders. Now both Connolly and Larkin were in Mountjoy.

On 3 September Murphy issued a statement on behalf of 404 employers outlining their determination to require all of their employees to sign the pledge against the I.T.G.W.U. It stated bluntly:

> We hereby pledge ourselves in the future not to employ any persons who continue to be members of the Irish Transport and General Workers' Union, and any person refusing to carry out our lawful and reasonable instructions or the instructions of those placed above them will be instantly dismissed no matter to what union they belong.[21]

The battle-lines had been drawn up. Many workers refused to sign and were accordingly dismissed. Within days over 20,000 workers had been locked out; taking account of dependants, it is estimated that some 100,000 people had been drawn into the dispute. On 7 September Connolly went on hunger-strike. The authorities finally yielded to protests, and Larkin was released on the 12th; Connolly was released on the 14th. The war, however, was only just beginning. Initially hopes were high among the workers; Connolly, in particular, thought defeat impossible if working-class solidarity was maintained. The backing of the British labour movement was essential, and much of Larkin's energy was spent attempting to generate radical support in Britain. In the days that followed this support was forthcoming. Foodships were sent, money was provided, and labour leaders from Britain made themselves available for mediation. The employers, however, remained intransigent, refusing to accept the results of an official inquiry, at which Connolly had represented the I.T.G.W.U. Liberty Hall (which had previously been a chop-house and hence had extensive cooking facilities) was turned into a soup-kitchen, providing meals and food parcels for the strikers and their families. The employers could afford their intransigence partly because large numbers of 'scab' workers were imported, and though Dublin port was virtually closed, workers in other ports and in Britain continued to handle what for Larkin and Connolly were 'tainted goods'. The employment of 'scabs' resulted in continuing street violence, which, among other things, resulted in the shooting to death of a young woman, Alice Brady, by a 'scab' worker. It was as a result of incidents such as these that, with the help of Captain Jack White, a person sympathetic to the union who had had military experience in the British army, Connolly and others founded the Irish Citizen Army, intended as an I.T.G.W.U. self-defence force.

The real solidarity that Larkin and Connolly were looking for was massive blacking of goods and, if necessary, sympathetic strike action, particularly in Britain. Although some few radical branches of British unions gave such support, not only did the leaders refuse to sanction and support such action, but at a special meeting of the British Congress of Trades Unions in the Albert Hall in London the Irish leaders were censured. Effectively, by the end of 1913 the battle was lost. A steady trickle of strikers began returning to work. In January 1914 Connolly put forward a face-saving plan that recommended a return to work 'pending a more general acceptance of the doctrine of tainted goods by the trade union world'.[22] By the first week of February he was publicly accepting defeat, bemoaning that the necessary 'brotherhood and self-sacrifice' had not been forthcoming and that the Irish workers had to 'eat the dust of defeat and betrayal'.[23]

1914–16: MILITANT NATIONALISM AND THE
EASTER RISING

I

With the acceptance of defeat in the Dublin lock-out, Connolly returned to normal union duties in Belfast. The year 1914, however, produced a confluence of events that were radically to change his life. The first set of events consisted in the growing militancy of the anti-Home Rule forces and what Connolly saw as the British government's almost complete capitulation to them. The Irish Parliamentary Party had already accepted a compromise qualification of the Home Rule Bill which would enable the inclusion of a provision for four Ulster counties to opt out temporarily on the basis of majority support. The Unionists, however, were not satisfied and demanded permanent partition. April 1914 witnessed the spectacular gun-running episode in which 36,000 rifles were landed at Larne and distributed, without opposition, to the Ulster Volunteers. When the government finally reacted, ordering troops from the Curragh to the north, fifty-seven officers threatened to resign rather than obey orders. Connolly became convinced that the government would concede permanent partition.[1] For many reasons he believed that this would be an unmitigated disaster of such an order that it 'should be resisted with armed force if necessary'.[2]

Connolly, of course, was not alone in his opposition to the dilution of Home Rule. Nationalists, both radical and moderate, reacted to the formation of the Ulster Volunteers by founding the Irish Volunteers under the leadership of Eoin MacNeill, Bulmer Hobson and Tom Clarke. The organisation was officially moderate, being pledged simply to the 'defence' of Home Rule gains, though both Clarke and Hobson were members of the secret extreme nationalist Irish Republican Brotherhood, which was to infiltrate the Volunteers in the coming years.

The major influence on Connolly's actions from 1914 onwards, however, was the outbreak of the First World War. As early as the 1890s Connolly had explicitly endorsed the classic Marxist position that war and imperialism in the modern world are fundamentally rooted in the protection of the commercial interests of capitalism.[3] Unlike many socialists, who on the outbreak of war reverted to a chauvinistic defence of their own country, Connolly consistently maintained a total opposition to the war, seeing it as the wanton slaughter of the workers of one country by the workers of another in the interests of that 'capitalist class which in its soulless lust for power and gold would bray the nations as in a mortar'.[4] Rather than 'socialists allowing themselves to be used in the slaughter of their brothers',[5] from the outset Connolly recommended militant action to ensure that the working class of Ireland would not be implicated in this 'carnival of murder'.[6] 'Starting thus, Ireland may yet set the torch to a European conflagration that will not burn out until the last throne and the last capitalist bond and debenture will be shrivelled on the funeral pyre of the last warlord'.[7] He was clearly adopting the policy that military action should be taken to 'rid this country once and for all from its connection with the Brigand Empire that drags us unwillingly into this war'.[8] From September onwards he initiated contact with members of the I.R.B. Publicly there was to be a concerted anti-war and, in particular, anti-conscription campaign. Secretly there was a tentative airing of the possibility of an insurrection. There is evidence to suggest that Connolly's daughter Nora acted as a secret emissary to some extreme nationalists in America as part of an attempt to secure German backing for an anti-British insurrection.

The other event of 1914 that was to have a major impact on Connolly's life was the 'temporary' resignation of Larkin as General Secretary of the I.T.G.W.U. and his emigration to America, leaving Connolly effectively in charge of the union. Larkin was not wholly in favour of Connolly's appointment, but enough support was mustered to get him to change his mind. With Larkin's departure for America in October, Connolly took over the running of the union, the editorship of the *Irish Worker*, and the leadership of the Irish Citizen Army. By all accounts, he

approached his job with great commitment and energy, reorganis-
ing the whole administration of Liberty Hall, down to getting the
building redecorated. His family remained in the house in Belfast,
while he stayed in Constance Markievicz's house in Rathmines,
Dublin.

While not at all withdrawing from ordinary union affairs—the
war resulted in something of a shortage of labour in Dublin, and
Connolly led many successful demands for higher wages by the
dockers, transport workers and railwaymen, among others—it is
probably true to say that his main orientation was towards a
possible military insurrection. This is nicely illustrated by the fact
that, shortly after taking over at Liberty Hall, he had a banner
hung across the front of the building proclaiming: 'We serve
neither King nor Kaiser but Ireland'. His articles in the *Irish
Worker* became more and more militant until eventually the
authorities acted to close it down. When he could no longer get it
printed in Ireland, he went in search of a press of his own. He
finally managed to acquire a fairly dilapidated one which he
installed in the basement of Liberty Hall, and from May 1915 he
continued producing the renamed *Workers' Republic*. By the end of
1915 the leaders of the I.R.B. had developed definite plans for an
insurrection at Easter in the following year. Fearing that
Connolly's growing bellicosity would jeopardise their plans, they
decided to establish direct contact with him. He was 'intercepted'
on the afternoon of 19 January 1916 outside Liberty Hall and was
'detained' in Chapelizod, a Dublin suburb, for three days.
Extensive negotiations took place between Connolly and the
I.R.B. leaders during which the terms of their co-operation in an
insurrection were agreed. From the end of January Connolly
began to prepare the Citizen Army for its role in the Easter
Rising. Liberty Hall became his military headquarters, where he
stockpiled weapons and medical supplies.

Most commentators on Connolly's life and thought recognise
that there is something of a problem in reconciling his seemingly
sudden conversion to the politics of insurrectionary nationalism
with his lifelong commitment to the patient building up of the
preconditions of a socialist revolution. There is a genuine
problem here. For Connolly had hitherto maintained a consistently hostile attitude towards political violence, and even in the

context of a struggle for socialism had derided the unfortunate insurrectionism of its early years. He had condemned the 'physical force' party in Irish politics,[9] and he had explicitly and consistently stated that national independence without socialism was simply not worth fighting for.[10] But here he now was planning a military insurrection with Irish nationalists who by no stretch of the imagination could be called 'socialist'. There were, however, several factors that explain Connolly's decision.

Firstly, there was the slaughter being perpetrated in the war. He was genuinely horrified at what he considered to be the greatest disaster to befall the world and at the criminal activities which were being carried out in the interest of capitalist lust for power and wealth. Consequently, even if nothing else was at stake, he seemed to think that Ireland's implication in this tragedy should be fought against, ridding 'this country once and for all from its connection with the Brigand Empire that drags us unwillingly into this war'.[11] Secondly, the speed with which socialist international brotherhood had collapsed into militant jingoistic nationalism led Connolly to the conclusion that what he had thought was a solid advance towards socialism in Britain and Europe was an illusion. He considered this really a 'pathetic failure'.[12] One consequence of this failure was his growing belief that capitalism, and in particular, Britain's imperialistic capitalism, was far from dead, with the implication that socialism in an Ireland politically subject to Britain was a complete impossibility. Hence national independence became a prerequisite for any advance towards socialism in Ireland.

Furthermore, Connolly had become convinced that the Irish Parliamentary Party under its leader John Redmond had sold 'Ireland to the Empire',[13] had settled for Ireland as a member of the Empire. As one consequence, whenever Ireland actually got Home Rule, it would not produce a level of independence necessary to provide the precondition for a development towards socialism. In addition, Connolly had come to believe that permanent partition would be inevitably conceded after the war, and this, he thought, would be utterly disastrous for the rights of the minority in Ulster. The partitioning of Ireland, and its continued inclusion within the Empire, would also ensure that the national question would remain at the centre of Irish politics,

resulting in the marginalisation of socialist issues and the destruc-
tion of the labour movement.[14]

Finally, a reading of the series of articles written by Connolly
in the *Workers' Republic* during 1915 would lead one to the conclusion that he actually did believe in the possibility of military
success.[15] In which case, he really could have hoped that (as
quoted above) 'Starting thus, Ireland may yet set the torch to a
European conflagration that will not burn out until the last
throne and the last capitalist bond and debenture will be shrivelled on the funeral pyre of the last warlord.'[16] A story is widely
told that illustrates that Connolly saw the planned insurrection as
the initial stage of a struggle for socialism. A week before the
rising he is said to have addressed a gathering of the Citizen Army
as follows:

> The odds are a thousand to one against us. If we win, we'll be
> great heroes; but if we lose, we'll be the greatest scoundrels
> the country has ever produced. In the event of victory, hold
> on to your rifles, as those with whom we are fighting may stop
> before our goal is reached. We are out for economic as well as
> political liberty.[17] *– workers*

II

The major events leading up to the planning of a military
insurrection, Connolly's own role in it, the chaos into which the
plan descended in the few days before its implementation and the
eventual outcome are all well known. As we have already noted,
the Military Council of the I.R.B. (Tom Clarke, Patrick Pearse,
Seán MacDermott, Joseph Plunkett and Eamonn Ceannt) had
decided on a rising on Easter Sunday 1916 and had informed
Connolly of this in late January, securing his participation. In
addition to the Citizen Army, which could only count on about
150 militantly committed members, the main force for the insurrection was to be the Irish Volunteers. This force, as we saw above,
had been founded in 1913 as a response to the formation of the
Ulster Volunteers. It initially had over 100,000 members, but when
John Redmond pledged Volunteer support for the British war
effort on a famous speech at Woodenbridge, a split occurred,

leaving the far larger body, renamed the National Volunteers, in Redmond's camp. The remaining Irish Volunteers themselves numbered only about 10,000. Even this 10,000, under the leadership of Professor Eoin MacNeill, were meant to be only a defensive force, a persuasive weight to protect the peacefully won gains of the Home Rule Act. However, its command structure had been infiltrated by the I.R.B.

The plan was that the whole force was to be called out on Easter Sunday, 23 April, for 'general manoeuvres', but would then be directed by the I.R.B. leaders into a real insurrection, the focal point being Dublin, but with extensive countrywide supporting action. The rural units were very poorly armed, and their effective participation depended upon the one piece of co-operation that the I.R.B., through the mediation of Roger Casement, had managed to secure from the German government, namely the landing of a shipment of arms. To ensure maximum compliance with orders, the I.R.B. leadership had persuaded MacNeill to countersign all orders. MacNeill was kept unaware of the I.R.B. conspiracy until almost the last moment, as he was opposed to military insurrection. He was to be got to agree to readying the Volunteers for armed resistance by convincing him that the British authorities were about to suppress the whole nationalist movement, arresting the leadership. This was to be done partly with the aid of the forged 'Castle Document', which contained the alleged plans for the arrests. It was at this point that a series of disasters struck, forcing a radical revision of the plans and effectively undermining whatever chance of success there might have been.

Firstly, owing to misunderstanding and a breakdown in communications, the arms-carrying ship, the *Aud*, was not met off the south coast as planned. Eventually, after being tracked down by the British navy, it was scuttled, with, of course, the complete loss of its cargo. Secondly, Casement, who had sailed from Germany on a submarine with two companions, was put ashore in Ballyheige Bay, but he was, in fact, soon located and arrested. Thirdly, MacNeill finally discovered around midnight on the Thursday before Easter that the I.R.B. had been planning an insurrection all along and that he had been duped. On Saturday 22 April he countermanded the general manoeuvres orders, made arrangements for the new orders to be distributed around the country, and delivered a copy of the countermand to the *Irish Independent* offices to be published in the Sunday edition.

When Connolly discovered the full extent of the disaster early on the Sunday morning, he immediately called a meeting of the Military Council in Liberty Hall at which it was decided to continue with the plans, the only alteration being a postponement from Sunday to Monday at noon. It was probably thought that, in the light of all that had happened, the British authorities would actually arrest the whole leadership of the militant nationalist movement, thus completely destroying it for the foreseeable future. It seems to be true, however, that Connolly radically revised his estimate of the possibility of success. William O'Brien reports that the last words Connolly said to him on Easter Monday in Liberty Hall were: 'We are going out to be slaughtered.' When O'Brien asked: 'Is there no chance of success?' Connolly replied: 'None whatever.'[18]

The actual plan for the military insurrection in Dublin centred on the seizing of the G.P.O. and the surrounding buildings in O'Connell Street. It was to become the seat of the Provisional Government which had been set up in accordance with the proclamation declaring the establishment of the Irish Republic. In addition, six other major areas were to be taken: Boland's Mills and the area around Clanwilliam Place and Grand Canal Street, St Stephen's Green, Jacob's biscuit factory, the buildings around the City Hall facing the main entrance to Dublin Castle, the Four Courts, about a mile up the River Liffey from O'Connell Street, and the South Dublin Union, which was a complex of hospital and poorhouse buildings, south-west of the Four Courts. There was a twofold purpose to the plan: firstly, to prevent access to the city centre from the major military barracks and the harbour at Kingstown (Dún Laoire); and secondly, to keep open a line of communication between Dublin and the country to the north-west. It was still hoped that, despite the countermanding of the orders, some support would be forthcoming from country areas. In the end that hope proved ill-founded in that practically nothing occurred outside of Dublin beyond a few minor skirmishes.

At 12 noon on Monday 24 April Connolly, who was named as Commandant-General of the rebel forces in Dublin, led a combined contingent of Citizen Army and Volunteer forces, accompanied by Pearse, Clarke, MacDermott and Plunkett, on the short march from Liberty Hall to the G.P.O. It and the surrounding buildings were captured and fortified, and the proclamation declaring the founding of the Irish Republic was read by Pearse, as President of the new republic and head of the Provisional Government. Connolly was declared Vice-President. Among other things in the declaration there are two statements that are thought to show Connolly's influence; the proclamation of 'the right of the people of Ireland to the ownership of Ireland', and the specific reference to election by 'the suffrages of all her men and women'. Meanwhile other insurgent units successfully seized their designated targets and dug in.

Despite an initial flurry of activity on O'Connell Street when a cavalry troop charged the G.P.O., losing three shot dead, the really intense fighting occurred at the various outposts around the city, particularly at Clanwilliam Place, Northumberland Road, the Four Courts and the South Dublin Union. It was Wednesday before the G.P.O. came under artillery bombardment, first from a gunboat, the *Helga*, moored on the Liffey, and then from artillery batteries located around Trinity College and D'Olier Street. The British army eventually invaded all the major rebel positions, and on Friday afternoon, with nearly all the surrounding buildings destroyed and the G.P.O. itself about to go up in flames, the decision was made to evacuate. The British had established a strong position about five hundred yards to the north on Parnell Street, and when, after evacuating the G.P.O. on Friday night, the leaders and the main contingent could get no further than a cottage in a lane off Moore Street about two hundred yards from the G.P.O., surrender was inevitable. After brief negotiations with the British General Lowe, Pearse and Connolly signed an unconditional surrender at four o'clock on Saturday 29 April. The ordinary men were confined to the grounds of the Rotunda Hospital, and the leaders were taken to Kilmainham Jail, except for Connolly himself, who had been seriously injured on the Thursday when a ricocheting bullet smashed his ankle. He was confined in the infirmary of Dublin Castle. The outlying units surrendered, and the rising was over.

By all accounts, as military commander of the rebel forces in Dublin, Connolly conducted himself with exemplary energy, dedication, concern for the men and women for whom he was responsible and great personal courage. He successfully concealed the initial flesh wound that he had received in his arm earlier on Thursday, except from the medical student who dressed it. He suffered great pain from his shattered ankle, as there were no adequate facilities or drugs to treat it properly. On the following day, however, he was joking and had himself put in a bed on castors so that he could be wheeled among his troops to encourage them.

Along with the other leaders of the rebellion, he was court-martialled and condemned to death. His daughter Nora has left a moving account of the last meeting between Connolly and his wife Lillie at which Nora was present.[19] Late on the night of 11 May, Nora and Lillie were brought to see Connolly in his infirmary room in Dublin Castle. When Connolly said: 'You know what this means, Lillie', she broke down in tears and said: 'But your beautiful life, James, your beautiful life.' Connolly replied: 'Well, hasn't it been a full life, and isn't this a good end?' A few hours later, early in the morning of 12 May, he was taken by military ambulance to Kilmainham Jail. Accompanied by a Brother Aloysius, whom he had asked to see a few times in the previous days and who had administered the Catholic sacraments to him, he was taken to the prison yard, where he was not, it appears, strapped to a chair, but placed seated on a rough wooden box. He was then executed by firing squad. Along with the other executed leaders he was buried in quicklime in Arbour Hill Barracks, where there is now a monument at the site of their common grave.

CONCLUSION

A full life it certainly was and, by any standards, a life full of significant achievement. Firstly, as Levenson notes,[1] there is what Connolly made of himself. A small squat man, standing five feet five, with bandy legs, and an accent that led him to refer to the cause to which he devoted his life as 'socy-ism', starting in the slums of Edinburgh with only the very basics of an education, he developed into a socialist thinker and writer of the first rank, capable of wrangling as an equal with conservative intellectuals such as Hilaire Belloc.[2] Despite a life taken up with trying to provide a living for his family, and engaging in an incessant struggle for the rights of the poor and the oppressed, he left behind him an impressive body of writing that is characterised by intellectual acuity, clarity, humour and style. His family were devoted to him, and among his colleagues his dedication, efficiency and singleminded commitment inspired high admiration and personal attachment. The Easter Rising was, in the short term, a failure, but it did stand at the beginning of a sequence of events that eventually resulted in an independent Ireland, though one that was partitioned and would not be considered by Connolly to be anywhere near the socialist workers' republic for which he had fought. On the other hand, many of the basic rights for ordinary men and women that he devoted his life to have in fact been secured. Finally, it is no mean achievement, even in a small country like Ireland, to have attained the status of a national hero and to have acquired a reputation of having been the very epitome of self-sacrificing socialist commitment.

NOTES

1

[1] C. Desmond Greaves, *The Life and Times of James Connolly* (London, 1961), p. 16.

[2] Austen Morgan, *James Connolly: A Political Biography* (Manchester, 1988); Lambert McKenna, *The Social Teachings of James Connolly*, ed. with commentary and introduction by Thomas J. Morrissey S.J. (Dublin, 1991) (originally published in 1920 by the Catholic Truth Society, Dublin); Andy Johnston, James Larragy and Edward McWilliams, *Connolly: A Marxist Analysis* (Dublin, 1990). These three books are good examples of radically different interpretations of Connolly that challenge, in different ways, his 'Marxism'.

[3] McKenna, *Social Teachings of James Connolly*, pp 43–53.

[4] James Connolly, *Collected Works* (2 vols, Dublin, 1987–8) (hereafter *CW*), i, 36.

[5] Quoted in Morgan, *Connolly*, p. 21.

[6] *CW*, ii, 383–4.

[7] Ibid., pp 401–2.

[8] Ibid., p. 212.

[9] Karl Marx, *Capital* (3 vols, Moscow, 1977) i, chs 1–11.

[10] *CW*, ii, 390.

[11] Ibid., p. 391.

[12] James Connolly, *Erin's Hope and The New Evangel* (Dublin & Belfast, 1972), p. 17.

[13] *CW*, ii, 212.

[14] Ibid., i, 337.

[15] Ibid., p. 36. For Marx's own formulation of the theory see Karl Marx, *Selected Writings*, ed. David McLellan (Oxford, 1977), pp 129–218.

[16] *CW*, ii, 212.

[17] Ibid., p. 388.

[18] Ibid., p. 385.

[19] On Marxism, Young Hegelianism and the critique of religion see Marx, *Selected Writings*, ed. McLellan. For a selection of writings discussing Marx on morality see David McLellan and Seán Sayers (eds), *Socialism and Morality* (London, 1990); see also David McLellan, *Marx before Marxism* (London, 1970).

[20] *CW*, ii, 371–82.

[21] Samuel Levenson, *James Connolly: A Biography* (London, 1973), p. 113.

2

[1] *CW*, i, 466–9.

[2] Ibid., p. 466.

[3] Ibid., p. 467.

[4] Ibid., p. 306.

[5] Ibid., ii, 212.

[6] Ibid., i, 307.

[7] Ibid., ii, 211.

[8] Ibid., i, 307.
[9] Ibid., p. 188.
[10] Ibid., p. 318.
[11] Ibid.
[12] Ibid., pp 310–15.
[13] Ibid., ii, 34–7.
[14] Ibid., i, 311.
[15] Ibid., pp 474–5.

3

[1] See *The Connolly—De Leon Controversy* (Cork, 1986).

[2] For Marx's position see 'Wages, Prices and Profit' in Karl Marx and Frederick Engels, *Selected Works* (Moscow, 1977), ii, 71–2.

[3] For a treatment of the issue that is highly critical of Connolly see Johnston, Larragy and McWilliams, *Connolly: A Marxist Analysis*.

[4] Quoted in Levenson, *Connolly*, p. 113.

[5] James Connolly, *Labour, Nationality and Religion* (Dublin, 1910).

[6] *Connolly—De Leon Controversy*, p. 8.

[7] Ibid., pp 30–31.

[8] Ibid., p. 46.

[9] Emmet O'Connor, *A Labour History of Ireland, 1824–1960* (Dublin, 1992), p. 44.

[10] *CW*, ii, 259–60.

[11] Ibid., p. 262.

[12] 'Old Wine in New Bottles' in James Connolly, *Selected Writings*, ed. P. Berresford Ellis (London, 1988), pp 175–6.

[13] *CW*, i, 315.

[14] Ibid., ii, 241.

[15] Ibid., pp 241–6.

[16] Ibid., p. 244.

[17] Connolly, *Erin's Hope and The New Evangel*, p. 28.

[18] Connolly, *Selected Writings*, ed. Ellis, p. 151.

[19] Ibid., p. 153.

[20] Ibid.

[21] Letter to Matheson, quoted in Levenson, *Connolly*, p. 147.

4

[1] *CW*, i, 36.
[2] Ibid., p. 37.
[3] Ibid., p. 22.
[4] Appendix, ibid., p. 509.
[5] Ibid., pp 116–32.
[6] Ibid., p. 184.
[7] Ibid., ii, 371–82.
[8] Ibid., p. 430.

[9] Ibid., i, 242–3. For a clear account of Connolly and the women's movement see W. K. Anderson, *James Connolly and the Irish Left* (Dublin, 1994), ch. 1.

[10] *CW,* i, 266.

[11] Ibid., pp 377–405.

[12] Connolly, *Selected Writings,* ed. Ellis, p. 150.

[13] *CW,* ii, 275.

[14] Ibid., i, 392–3.

[15] Ibid., p. 386.

[16] Ibid., pp 385–6.

[17] See, for example, James L. Hyland, *Democratic Theory: The Philosophical Foundations* (Manchester, 1995).

[18] A very accessible account, with reprints of contemporary documents and archival photographs, can be found in Curriculum Development Unit, *Dublin 1913: A Divided City* (Dublin, 1982).

[19] Quoted in Levenson, *Connolly,* p. 202.

[20] *Dublin 1913: A Divided City,* p. 84.

[21] Ibid., p. 83.

[22] Quoted in Levenson, *Connolly,* p. 246.

[23] *CW,* ii, 324.

5

[1] *CW,* i, 438.

[2] Ibid., p. 391.

[3] Ibid., ii, 25–6.

[4] Ibid., p. 42.

[5] Ibid., p. 41.

[6] Ibid., p. 90.

[7] Ibid., i, 416.

[8] Ibid., p. 415.

[9] Ibid., pp 335–40.

[10] Ibid., ii, 211.

[11] Ibid., i, 415.

[12] Ibid., ii, 60.

[13] Ibid., i, 443.

[14] Ibid., ii, 39.

[15] Ibid., pp 451–83.

[16] Ibid., i, 416.

[17] Greaves, *Connolly,* p. 403.

[18] William O'Brien, 'Introduction' to 'Labour and Easter Week' in *CW,* ii, 21.

[19] Nora Connolly O'Brien, *Portrait of a Rebel Father* (Dublin, 1935), pp 20–32.

Conclusion

[1] Levenson, *Connolly,* pp 334–5.

[2] Ibid., p. 218.

SELECT BIBLIOGRAPHY

Connolly's Writings

Nearly all of Connolly's published writings, including his three longest pieces, *Labour in Irish History, Labour Nationality and Religion,* and *The Reconquest of Ireland,* can now be found in James Connolly, *Collected Works* (2 vols, New Books Publications, Dublin, 1987–8).

The most important exceptions are the following: James Connolly, *Socialism Made Easy* (Chicago, 1908), and *Erin's Hope: The End and the Means* and *The New Evangel* (Dublin, 1972). For Connolly's controversy with Daniel De Leon, *The Connolly—De Leon Controversy* (Cork Workers, Cork, 1976) reproduces the material originally published in the American Socialist Labor Party's journal, the *Weekly People,* in 1904.

Secondary Works

There have been numerous full-length studies of Connolly's life and thought, many of them written from very distinctive political partisan perspectives. A notable exception is the recent work by W. K. Anderson, *James Connolly and the Irish Left* (Dublin, 1994), which contains an extremely exhaustive bibliography. The others that I have found most useful are:

Allen, Kieran, *The Politics of James Connolly* (London, 1990)

Greaves, C. Desmond, *The Life and Times of James Connolly* (London, 1961)

Johnston, Andy, Larragy, James, and McWilliams, Edward, *Connolly: A Marxist Analysis* (Irish Workers' Group, Dublin, 1990)

Levenson, Samuel, *James Connolly: A Biography* (London, 1973)

Morgan, Austen, *James Connolly: A Political Biography* (Manchester, 1988)

Ransom, Bernard, *Connolly's Marxism* (London, 1980)

In addition to the above, the following works place Connolly's life in differing important contexts:

Caulfield, Max, *The Easter Rebellion* (Dublin, 1963)

Curriculum Development Unit, *Dublin 1913: A Divided City* (Dublin, 1989)

Keogh, Dermot, *The Rise of the Irish Working Class* (Belfast, 1982)

O'Connor, Emmet, *A Labour History of Ireland, 1824–1960* (Dublin, 1992)

Two important selections should also be mentioned:

Ellis, P. Berresford (ed.), *James Connolly: Selected Writings* (London, 1988)

Edwards, Owen Dudley, and Ransom, Bernard (eds), *James Connolly: Selected Political Writings*, (London, 1973)

There is, finally, a long personal memoir written by Connolly's daughter Nora:

Nora Connolly O'Brien, *James Connolly: Portrait of a Rebel Father* (Dublin, 1935)

NOTES

Closeness of his family + own poverty for a
time, able to understand plight of the
workers.

HISTORICAL ASSOCIATION OF IRELAND

Life and Times Series

●

'The Historical Association of Ireland is to be congratulated for its **Life and Times** Series of biographies. They are written in an authoritative, accessible and enjoyable way'

History Ireland

'Promises to be an important and valuable series'

Irish Historical Studies

'A very useful series and much to be welcomed by teachers'

Stair

●

No. 1 — HENRY GRATTAN
by JAMES KELLY

'The series has set a rigorous standard with this short study'

Books Ireland

'An up-to-date and sane account of the main aspects of Grattan's career'

K. Theodore Hoppen, Irish Historical Studies

No. 2 — SIR EDWARD CARSON
by ALVIN JACKSON

'A scintillating essay in reappraisal'

K. Theodore Hoppen, Irish Historical Studies

'Jackson's splendid *Sir Edward Carson*'

Irish Times

No. 3 — EAMON DE VALERA
by PAURIC TRAVERS

'A good short summary of a very long political life'

Stair